THE TROUBLE
WITH GRAMARY

The Trouble with Gramary

by Betty Levin

GREENWILLOW BOOKS, New York

*Grateful acknowledgment is made for permission
to reprint excerpts from the following works:*

"Blueberry Hill," by A. Lewis, V. Rose, L. Stock. Copyright © 1940 by Chappell & Co., Inc. and Sovereign Music Co. Copyright renewed. International copyright secured. All rights reserved. Used by permission.

"Maine," from *Relations: Selected Poems 1950–1985*, by Philip Booth. Copyright © 1960 by Philip Booth. By permission of Viking Penguin Inc.

"Stormy Weather" ("Keeps Rainin' All the Time"), by Harold Arlen and Ted Koehler. Copyright © 1933 Mills Music, Inc. Copyright renewed 1961 Arko Music Corp. and Mills Music, Inc. International copyright secured. All rights reserved. Used by permission.

"That Old Black Magic," by Johnny Mercer and Harold Arlen. Copyright © 1942 by Famous Music Corporation. Copyright renewed 1969 by Famous Music Corporation.

LIBRARY OF CONGRESS CATALOGING-IN-PUBLICATION DATA
Levin, Betty.
The trouble with Gramary/by Betty Levin.
   p.   cm.
Summary: Merkka's longing for a solid conventional existence
is threatened by the art projects of her stubborn sculptor
grandmother, whose scrap metal collection offends the other
citizens in their small Maine village.
ISBN 0-688-07372-7
[1. Grandmothers—Fiction.   2. Maine—Fiction.
3. Sculptors—Fiction.   4. Refuse and refuse disposal—Fiction.
5. Recycling (Waste)—Fiction.]   I. Title.
PZ7.L5759Tr 1988   [Fic]—dc19   87-22702   CIP   AC

FOR BARBARA AND SUSAN

IN MEMORY OF

PAUL AND PAUL AND ALVIN

CONTENTS

THE TROUBLE
WITH GRAMARY

CHAPTER 1:

Weather Coming

*The day the trouble started we were out on Grace Island
to pick up Mrs. Cope's laundry. Usually Gramary and
Mrs. Cope visit while Ben and I go beachcombing. But
this afternoon Mrs. Cope was away for her operation to
fix her knee. So Gramary had no one to talk to, but she
waited anyhow, because she knew that Charlie Budge
was over on the other side of the island and up to
something. She was some riled that he hadn't let her in
on it.*

*Ben tried to get Gramary to come beachcombing with
us. Every time we go to Grace Island Ben collects plastic
stuff that washes up on the shore. Mrs. Cope pays him a
penny for each detergent bottle or milk carton he cleans
off her beach. If he gets tonic bottles and brings them
home, he can turn them in for a nickel at Stan's Market.*

Gramary eased herself down on a dry rock and

heaved a big sigh. "Not today," she said. "I'm tired." She was all spread out on that rock, her faded overalls sort of puffed up around her.

"You never come. Why are you tired?"

"I'm old."

Ben said, "No, you're not," and he stomped away to hunt for plastic by himself.

"What's the matter with him?" I asked.

"He doesn't like to think of me getting old and dying," Gramary answered.

Her saying that stopped the words in my mouth. For the first time she was talking to me woman to woman. When something like that happens, you want to handle it right. You try too hard to act grown up. I wanted to sound matter-of-fact, like her, but when I opened my mouth, all the dumbest words inside me fell out at once. I said, "When you die, I might make everyone call me Mary. Is that all right? Is it fair to use your name if you're dead and can't do anything about it?"

"It's fair," Gramary said. "You can use it now if you like."

I shook my head. "People would think I was trying to copy you."

"I doubt that," Gramary told me. "You didn't choose the name. You've just as much right to it as I have."

I thought that over a moment. Everyone calls me Merkka, which means Little Mary. Our lobster boat is named Little Mary too. But the whole town of Ledgeport knows that Gramary is Mary Weir. I said, "I think I'll wait until you're dead." Suddenly I felt awful that I'd put it that way. But Gramary didn't seem put out.

"That might be some time," she warned.
"That's all right," I told her. "I can wait."
"Good," said Gramary. "I'm relieved to know it."

They sat there long enough for Ben to make two trips with plastic junk.

Merkka picked Styrofoam from the underside of a thwart. By the time the ocean had thrust it onto the rocks and the tide had pushed it farther up the shore, the wood was badly splintered. That didn't matter to Merkka, though. She just wanted the Styrofoam part to bring home.

Finally Gramary heaved herself up. "Well," she grumbled, "if Charlie's got himself in trouble, it's his own fault for not telling me." She picked up the sack of sheets and towels. Ben gathered his plastic finds. Merkka clutched her yellowed Styrofoam.

After they reached the fancy new float Charlie Budge had made for the island, Gramary took her time stowing everything aft in the *Little Mary*. She looked all around. It seemed late suddenly. The air felt heavy, but there was no true fog and hardly any wind.

"Weather coming," she remarked as she started up the engine.

"A storm?" asked Merkka. She pulled the stern line inboard but kept her eye on Gramary.

"Don't know. The wind's going east." Gramary squinted over the gray water. Tinker's Island seemed to be shrinking before their eyes. Toward the mainland the Porcupines were just barely visible, and beyond them Indian Point hardly showed at all.

"Funny," Gramary said as they chugged out into Grace Narrows.

Gramary had lived through so much weather that for her it was something to measure with her eye and her ear, even if she faced it head on. Dad was like that, too, though he seemed more willing to change his plans. Mom said it was because he had one eye on the weather and the other on his family. He would never let a storm take him by surprise.

"Maybe it's a hurricane." Ben spoke eagerly. "Maybe the waves will come right over Water Street and into Stan's Market."

"Will they?" Merkka asked. "Is it?"

Gramary said there was a lot of warning for hurricanes nowadays, so it couldn't be that. Ben was disappointed. He lived for the day that something exciting came along, something dangerous like all those stories they heard on the wharf. Merkka tried to sound disappointed too. Not a hurricane. Not today.

She knew that someday such a storm would come, not an ordinary nor'easter, but an immense swelling of sea that could pick up boats as big as the deep-water trawlers, tip them on end, and suck them to the bottom. Sooner or later a storm would fill Ledgeport harbor and rip mooring lines and topple the monument and float all the summer yachts off their cradles. And rise up like a giant with Ed's boat shed on one shoulder and Merkka's home on the other. That day would come when the sea would shrug its mighty shoulders to rid itself of its burden. One shrug, and the long boat shed that spanned the drop between Water Street and the pier would slide under the waves. Another shrug, and the harbor side of Merkka's house would collapse, walls buckling, ceilings caving in, floors giving way. Sooner or later, but not today.

"Sing!" Merkka prompted.

"'Don't know why, there's no sun up in the sky, stormy weather . . . !'" The song came forth in a deep, resounding voice that might have passed for a hymn, except that it was one of those love songs from the olden days. Merkka thought God might pay more attention to a prayer song, like "Amazing Grace"; Gramary always sang that as they approached Grace Island. What they needed now was a hymn for coming home.

"Sing 'Eternal Father,'" she commanded.

Gramary obliged. Merkka and Ben joined in: "'Whose arm doth bind the restless wave. . . .'" Merkka's spirits rose. She could see past Indian Point now and all the way to Limeburner Point. "'O hear us when we cry to Thee, for those in peril on the sea.'" They never sang hymns like prayers; they belted them out. That was Gramary's way of singing. But Merkka believed it was the words that counted. There would be no storm. Soon they would be home safe and sound.

CHAPTER 2:

Something Overboard

*Night comes up from the sea just the way it comes down
from the sky. First Grace Island goes black like the
water. Then the new pier shrinks into the darkness.
Gramary never looks back, though. She looks ahead
toward Ledgeport, always with an eye out for other
boats and drift. She never speeds home. Night coming,
even a storm, and Gramary just goes chugging along as
though we had all the time in the world.*

"There's Charlie Budge!" Ben shouted over the engine racket.
Gramary stopped singing.

"He's going to pass us," cried Ben. "Gramary, hurry."

"He always passes us," Merkka reminded Ben. "His boat can
go twice as fast as ours."

"Please!" Ben pleaded. "Race him."

But Gramary just glanced back at Charlie's runabout scud-
ding over the water. She had to turn quickly, because they
were coming up to the monument that stood before the break-

water and warned people away from the underwater ledges and the old wreck stuck on them. It was so dark by now that only the white paint at the base of the monument pole showed clearly. Still, you could go all the way up to it safely. You just wouldn't want to miss it in a fog or at night.

"Where's Charlie Budge now?" Ben wondered out loud.

Gramary shut down the throttle and turned the wheel hard. The *Little Mary* cut through its own wake.

"What are you doing that for?" Ben asked.

"To see where Charlie's got to," Gramary told him. "At the rate he was going, he ought to be inside the breakwater already. But he didn't pass us."

"What are we going to do?" Ben climbed onto the foredeck and peered out. "Maybe he hit something. If he hit something going that fast, what would happen to him?"

Gramary frowned. "We'll have a listen first. Maybe we'll hear him coming." She brought the boat up alongside the monument and threw a line around the pole. She fished the end of the line up with the gaff and let the boat hang off so that anyone else coming in would see the monument and find the way. When she cut the engine, Merkka heard, clear as anything, the creak and grind of a winch hauling up something on the dock. She heard a truck roaring uphill and then she saw its headlights on Landing Road. She heard a horn honking from over by the town wharf. Someone shouted and someone else shouted back. These were all town noises. There was no sign of Charlie's boat speeding toward them.

Then Ben heard something. "It sounds like us," he whispered.

Merkka and Gramary heard it too. Charlie Budge poking along.

Ben sighed and slipped back into the cockpit. "We don't have to rescue him then."

Gramary muttered something unkind about Charlie Budge fooling around. "We'll just lay here and be quiet till he goes by," she said. "If he's gone and got his drive shaft tangled in pot warp, charging around like he does, we'll just act like we don't know."

They waited for Charlie Budge to bring his runabout past the monument and on around the seawall. He never noticed the *Little Mary*. He was too busy fussing around in his boat. As soon as he was between them and the harbor they could see that he was yanking at something bulky. He turned it and yanked again. Then he picked it up, a sort of huge bundle, and heaved it over the side. It made a big plop, followed by a splash. After that he revved up his outboard and steamed into the harbor.

"What was that?" cried Ben. "You see that?"

"Probably trash." Gramary sounded disgusted. "Too lazy to bury it out there. That's why he slowed down. So no one would see him dumping it in the harbor."

"It's outside the breakwater," Ben pointed out.

"Just barely."

"If I find it tomorrow and there's plastic stuff in it, will Mrs. Cope pay me?"

Gramary cast off from the monument and sent Merkka aft to bring in the line. Then she told Ben that Mrs. Cope paid him to clean up the shore of Grace Island, not the whole Maine coast. Ben started to argue, but Merkka, coiling the line at the stern, stopped listening. She was looking at something that bobbed in the water. She almost shouted to Gramary to turn back so they could pick it up, only it didn't look like a bag of trash. Maybe it was just a harbor seal.

Merkka tried to keep her eyes on it as it spun and spun and slowly curved out of sight. Her hands were raised, as if to stop it. And then, for an instant, she caught sight of it again, a blob circling in the water. Circling, not drifting with the tide. She wanted to believe that it was a seal following them for the fun of it, but her stomach felt pinched as if giant lobster claws had hold of her. Everything looked queer, the stern line like a wet snake, her own hands greeny-white and creepy. Then she realized that the *Little Mary* had rounded the breakwater. It was town and harbor lights that turned everything funny colors.

Ahead of them Charlie Budge seemed to change his direction. His runabout swerved as if to head back into the bay. Then it swerved again and made for its mooring. Gramary kept a steady course until the *Little Mary* slid alongside Ingalls' float.

Dad was waiting for them, wondering what had kept them out so long. Gramary tossed him the big bag of laundry.

All of a sudden Merkka saw it happening again, saw Charlie Budge slinging something overboard and the something moving in the black water outside the breakwater. Dad's big hand took hold of Merkka's and hauled her up beside Ben. Dad smelled of fish and baked potatoes and fuel.

Merkka walked up the ramp and then leaned against a wharf pile until her stomach stopped tumbling around. The lobster had let go of her. But sometimes when she'd been on the water everything on shore kept moving for a while. She bent her knees. She could feel the wharf dip like a boat under her feet. She couldn't tell whether it was moving outside or inside of her.

CHAPTER 3:

A Dog on the Wreck

I've seen pictures of houses on stilts over water. The people who live in them are nearly naked. You never see them in sweaters and foul-weather gear, because it's always warm where they are. So it doesn't matter living like that.

Our house reminds me of those others. If you came in from Water Street, you'd never guess that the living room and the upstairs are over the harbor. First you walk through a little room with jackets and slickers hanging from the wall and boots under them. Then you're in the kitchen, with the bathroom to one side and the door to the outside stairs across from it. But if you keep going straight, you end up in the living room, which is also Gramary's room. The inside stairs go up, turn, and go up again. There's a middle space. Mom and Dad have the room on the left; Ben and I have the room on the right.

*The outside stairs from the kitchen go down to the
yard. You have to hold on to the rail because they're so
steep. The yard is where Dad keeps his fishing things
and Gramary has her welding business. Dad buys and
sells bait, which he keeps in a shack where the old
steamboat landing used to be. It smells some ripe in
there, what with the barrels of herring and redfish for
the lobster traps, but we're used to it. In the winter the
traps are stacked high and lashed down. In the summer
there's generally one or two rowboats hauled up on the
shore and tipped over.*

*Gramary used the shack and the traps and the boats
long before Dad did. When she taught him and Uncle
Henry all about lobster fishing, she took to welding and
making things. That's why you see parts of old cars and
trucks and tractors all over the yard. You see marine
gear, too, things like dragger doors and that tall rig Ed
Ingalls used to step masts with and set engines down
into boats before Gramary made him a new one that
works with a hydraulic lift. You also see the old
weapons carrier from the war that Grampa was
wounded in. All the parts have been replaced so often
that Dad says it's entirely homemade now. The school
bus is newer, although Gramary has been working on it
as long as I can remember.*

*Anyway, those are some of the things you look out on
from our windows. When you're down in the yard, you
can watch the tide come in right under the living room.
The sea slaps against the bottom of our house.*

*My best friend, Lucy Starobin, likes coming to our
place. Sometimes we go over to Ed Ingalls' wharf next*

door. We sit with our legs dangling off the edge of the
dock and listen to the wharf gossip. Once we heard old
Reggie Ingalls tell about the night the tide came
sneaking up on the town and carried off the steamboat
landing. "Undermined the pilings and the cross braces
first. I saw it happen. After the storm was all blowed
out. That sea fetched up the back way, through
Muskeag Cove. All of the lower end of Landing Road
was flooded."

Lucy says she needs to know these things because
she's going to be a sea captain. Since she wants to run a
sailing boat, she's planning on having one of those
trippers, a schooner that takes paying guests.

Lucy has it all figured out, but I still don't know what
I want to do when I grow up. I only know that I want to
live on solid ground in a house like Lucy's. Her house
sits on huge granite slabs and makes me think of
Gramary's hymn, "How firm a foundation. . . ." You'd
never worry about the weather there because it's kept
outside. No amount of wind or tide could push the sea
under that rock.

The day after the late return from Grace Island, Merkka went
home from school with Lucy Starobin. Lucy's brother, Jay, let
them listen to some of his records. By the time Merkka left, it
was nearly dark. She ran all the way down Landing Road to
Water Street and got home just when Mom did. Mom had been
working late at the fish plant again and was in a bad mood.

They were ready for supper when Dad came in through the
side door. He stopped to kick off his sea boots; then he padded
over to the table in his socks. He ate all his meatloaf and
mashed potatoes without saying a word. Merkka knew that

only meant he was hungry, not crabby like Mom. Ben was telling him how much money he'd made returning bottles to
Stan's Market. Merkka was just half listening when Dad
stretched, pushed back his chair, and said, "There's a dog on
the wreck."

"On the wreck?" said Ben.

"You mean stuck?" Gramary asked.

"Looks that way. At least until the tide comes up."

Merkka couldn't imagine anything stranded out there. Not
even the seals got up on that slimy black hulk.

"Can we get it?" asked Ben.

Dad said he doubted it. Someone had tried, but couldn't get
close enough, not with the sea making up outside.

After supper Ben watched TV, but Merkka couldn't think
about anything but that dog. Finally she asked Dad if he would
try to get it off the wreck.

Dad said, "Dogs can get themselves in awful scrapes."

But that was no answer. "You have to try," she told him.

"Have to?"

"Dad!"

"What's the magic word?"

"Please, please. It's not the dog's fault it's out there. You
can't just leave it."

"How do you know it's not its fault?"

"It can't be. No dog would be on a place like that if there was
anything else it could do."

Dad thought a moment. "All right," he said. "If it's still there
in the morning, I'll see what I can do."

"You mean someone else may rescue it?"

Dad shook his head. "I just think it might not be there by
tomorrow."

Mom said quickly, "It might rescue itself. It might wait for
high tide and just jump in the water and swim ashore."

Merkka looked at Dad. "Is that what you mean?"

Merkka's parents spoke to each other without words. Then

Dad said, "That's right. It could be waiting on the tide. The tide might help it off."

Ben, who was still watching TV, said, "It will drown."

"It's none of your business," Merkka shouted at him. "You're not even thinking about the dog anyway. Dad's talking to *me*, and he didn't say anything about drowning."

"It's probably drowning right this minute," said Ben, his eyes fixed on the TV screen.

Merkka ran upstairs. She kicked aside some of Gramary's homemade tractor toys that Ben always left lying all over their room. Later Mom came upstairs and told Merkka to understand that Ben was upset about the dog too.

"Then he shouldn't mention drowning," Merkka retorted. "He shouldn't even say it."

Mom said, "I'm too tired for this," and went to her own room. When Dad came up, he stopped to speak to Merkka too. He said that if she promised not to worry anymore and got a good night's sleep, he'd do his best. He might even get after Russell Leeward, who was harbormaster. Maybe Russ would help out.

Merkka promised. But she lay in bed worrying anyhow. The sea was making such a racket she didn't even hear Ben come into the room. He made a lot of noise too. Merkka knew he wanted her to talk to him the way she usually did before they went to sleep. But she kept her eyes squeezed shut, against him, against what she had seen the night before or thought she had seen, that blob going round in circles out there in the black, shining water.

CHAPTER 4:

Nightdark

Before I started first grade I spent most of my time with Gramary the way Ben does now. When we weren't in the yard fixing something for one of Gramary's friends, we were over on the wharf where sooner or later all those friends turned up. Summer was different, with weekly trips to Grace Island for the laundry, and the harbor full of sailboats and stinkpots and people buying lobster off Dad. Lucy Starobin's family started out like that, summer people from away. Now Mr. Starobin teaches English in the Regional High School and Mrs. Starobin teaches music here.

In the winter the wharf is practically deserted, but there's always someone inside Ed Ingalls' boat shed. Mrs. Blanche Ingalls comes down midday with Ed's dinner, and often there's enough to feed the whole waterfront. Outside the wind can be howling, and

*inside we're having a picnic. Ed always dumps the
leftover spaghetti or fish chowder through the hole in the
floor for the gulls or the tide, whichever gets there first.*

*That's how I got in the habit of listening. I'd hear
when the lobsters were thinning out. I'd hear about
what Norman Gray caught in his drag that looked like
something off one of those Russian factory ships that
used to fish offshore. Some of the talk was about prices
and fish auctions, things I didn't understand very well,
or about someone named Marilyn who was in Sonny's
car that night it turned over in Brackett's cornfield, or
about double-purpose winches or the high cost of fish
finders or the scarcity of groundfish because the
Canadians were getting them.*

What stayed in Merkka's mind were the disaster stories. There
was always some boat that went on the rocks and broke up
before it could be salvaged. Once in a while Norman Gray or
someone else who unloaded fish down the coast would bring
back some terrible news of a man overboard. Norm would recollect the trawler he worked on years ago and how a man was
lost in rough seas. Norm described it the same way every time,
so Merkka knew the account by heart: "Right before my eyes.
Them cables jumped, slapped the deck, the net hung up on
bad bottom. We backed till it was freed, then pulled forward.
And pow! The cable cracked like a whip. He was all wrapped
up in his yellow apron, that thing flapping like ocean pout on
the deck. Must've been the apron caught. There was this flash
of yellow, and he was flying up over. Then he was gone."

Someone would always ask, "Couldn't see him? Couldn't
hear him yell?"

"We was so close to that ledge all we could hear was sea
breaking, and them winches squealing, and the wind. No, we

never heard a sound off him. Young fellow, too, just married and a baby coming."

Every word stayed with Merkka. She would picture the scene as clearly as if she were seeing it replayed on television. Except that it wasn't the big stern trawler Norm used to go out on before he got his own dragger. It was the *Little Mary* she saw bobbing and wallowing the way it did in rough water while Dad hauled up the traps and Ben and Merkka slid on bait all over the cockpit. Dad didn't wear a yellow apron, though. He wore his seaboots, usually turned down, and his rubber overalls and a foul-weather jacket. Merkka wished Dad didn't keep his jacket open and flapping.

She never followed the scene through to its horrifying end. She couldn't. The last part of Norm's story always got stuck, like the trawl net hung up on bad bottom. Merkka knew that if she were brave enough to back up and take her time, the awful outcome, like the net, would rise up and be revealed. She would grow cold with the nearness of it, cold as the seawater that in the best of times could numb your hands and stop your breath.

There was always the tide beneath the house and the wreck outside to remind her of that scene. Once that wreck had been a ship. People had gone to sea on it. Now it lay like a corpse that refused to stay buried. Every low tide showed it to the living world. How could a dog survive there through a flood tide? If the dog backed away from the coming sea, it could easily slip between the rotted timbers and be trapped. If it plunged into the water, could it make it to shore, or would it circle in confusion until it was too exhausted to swim anymore?

Merkka thought morning would never come. She meant to get up when she heard Dad going out in the dark the way he always did, but when she finally fell asleep she missed hearing him. By the time she woke, a dull gray light surrounded the house. There wasn't any rain yet, though once in a while she could hear the wind spitting at her window. By now, she thought, Dad would be easing the *Little Mary* around the shoals and hauling traps.

Mom, who was just getting ready to leave for work when Merkka came down to the kitchen, was saying to Gramary that she hoped Dad would be back inside before it started to blow.

"He'd better not forget the dog," Merkka said.

Mom sent her a heavy look. "You think more of a dog than your own father?"

Gramary told Mom, "Sam would never do anything foolish; you know that."

Merkka went off to school feeling awful for what she'd said and even more awful because she still hoped Dad would keep his promise.

It was a long day. The darkness came like night at the wrong time. Even though this was already the second week of school, no one felt like doing much. There was a waiting feeling, a sort of expectancy.

Only nothing happened except workbook time. Merkka looked at her page, and then she looked out the window. When Miss Guarino came to check up on her, Merkka hadn't done a thing. Miss Guarino said she was surprised, which meant she was disappointed. She told Merkka to take the workbook home and be all caught up by tomorrow.

Lucy was impressed. "It's like Jay's homework," she told Merkka. "When you're in high school you get all kinds of stuff to do every night."

Today Merkka went straight home. She was hoping Dad had come in early, but he wasn't back yet. Gramary remarked that it was sensible of Merkka to get right inside on a day like this.

"What kind of day?" Merkka snapped. "It isn't any kind of day. I have homework."

"Let's see," said Ben. "I want to see the homework."

"Just don't drool on it or anything," she told him as she slammed the workbook down on the kitchen table. She turned back to the door.

"Where are you going now?" asked Gramary.

"To the dock," she said. "To meet Dad."

"He may be awhile. Be back before dark."

"It is dark," Merkka shot back. "It's been dark for hours."

Gramary said evenly, "You know what I mean. By night-dark."

"I'm going too," Ben chimed in.

"No!" cried Merkka.

"Stay with me," Gramary suggested to him.

"I've been with you. I want to be with Merkka now."

As Merkka shut the door, she heard Gramary telling Ben, "Merkka needs a spell by herself."

She waited on the wharf until she saw Spike Breslaw heading in. Then she ran down to the float and called out to him. "Seen Dad? He's getting the dog off the wreck."

"Nope," Spike shouted back. "Dog's still there."

Merkka tore up the ramp and around Ed's boat shed to Water Street. She ran right past her own house and turned down Landing Road and out to Weir Cove. By the time she reached the great pile of boulders where the breakwater started from the shore, she was stumbling and breathless. You didn't climb out on it unless you watched every step. Merkka knew that. She had been on it often, only always in the summer with the sun shining and other kids around and yachts everywhere. It was different now.

Slowly, feeling her way, she began to climb along the rocky spine of the breakwater. She wanted to get far enough out to see the wreck, but soon it would be nightdark. The sea was heaving against the rockface outside. It smelled of low tide. Maybe Dad was out there waiting for the ebb slack before approaching the wreck.

On she went, though it was tough going and sometimes she dropped to her hands and knees. Well before the end of the breakwater she caught sight of a lobster boat going past the monument. Even if it was Dad, it was too dark to recognize the boat. She only saw its lights bouncing up and down as they moved toward the inner harbor.

She stopped and faced seaward. Nightdark had already swallowed the wreck. She could only guess what it must look like now with the sea slopping against it. Was the dog there, still clinging to the slime-covered wood? Or was it on its way, on that lobster boat heading in?

Making her way as quickly as she could, she scraped and slid back along the breakwater. She couldn't see at all anymore. She had to tell herself she wasn't stranded, though; she was connected with the land. After she finally clambered down from the rock pile on the shore, she was so relieved that she plunged toward Landing Rock and tripped. She fell with a jolt on one knee and the palms of her hands. She had to sit a moment in the swamp grass then, holding herself and sucking in her breath. After that she took her time to find the road and to keep on it going home.

She could hear arguing before she even opened the door. When she stepped inside, they all fell silent, so she knew the argument had been about her. Then Dad spoke up. He didn't want her out after dark in bad weather. Mom, glaring at Gramary, said Merkka shouldn't even have gone out at all.

Merkka didn't dare ask about the dog then. She was afraid they might guess where she had been. She just picked up her workbook and took it up to her room.

As soon as she heard Gramary coming, she turned on the lamp and opened the workbook. Gramary walked into the room and scooped up Ben's tractors and dumped them in the lobster box. Merkka bent over the workbook, pencil in hand. Gramary spoke to her from the door.

"It would be a good idea to change your pants before you come down to supper."

Merkka swiveled on the bed and clutched her sodden knee, but Gramary was no longer there. Merkka heard her clumping down the stairs.

Probably Dad and Mom had been too upset to see what Gramary had noticed. Merkka dashed into the hall where the clean laundry was stacked and found a pair of jeans to change into. She rolled the wet ones, still grimy with sand and swamp grass, and shoved them under her bed.

At supper she kept waiting for Dad to mention the dog, but he seemed to have other things on his mind. Merkka decided to eat three more forkfuls of noodles. Then she would tell him what Spike had said about the dog still being out on the wreck.

But he spoke first. "Tried to pry that dog loose, but it wouldn't come. Just snapped at the pole."

"You used a pole? You must've scared it."

Dad shrugged. "It won't let anyone help it. I got Russ Leeward out there. Of course, he had to get a photographer to come take a picture for the paper." Dad laughed. "Wish they'd got a shot of Russ tipping over backward to get out of the dog's way when he tried to pick it off."

"What's going to happen then?" Merkka asked him.

Dad shrugged again. "It can't last much longer. It looks half dead already."

Merkka glanced from one face to another. Mom just shook her head. She got up to clear away the plates.

Dad said, "I know I promised. I did try. I guess the dog doesn't want to be saved."

Merkka jumped up from the table. "We can't just leave it there!"

Mom declared, "I've heard enough about that dog. Enough."

Dad reached around her and caught Merkka in his other arm. "Come on, you two. Storm's brewing outside. Let's keep it peaceful in here."

After that there was nothing more Merkka could say. She went back upstairs to her workbook. Even Ben was afraid to speak out. He was in bed and asleep before Merkka had finished her homework. Mom and Dad went to bed early, too, but Merkka kept the light on and listened to the windows rattle.

Much later she remembered about her wet jeans. When she pulled them out from under her bed, some of the Styrofoam she kept there came out too. She shoved the Styrofoam back out of sight. Pretty soon she would borrow some more of Dad's duct tape and fasten the Styrofoam to the bottom of her bedsprings.

She carried the pants down to the washing machine in the bathroom. Then she stayed awhile in the kitchen. It always felt more solid there.

Gramary called softly, "You want to come in my bed?"

Merkka gripped the table. "No."

She heard Gramary shifting herself on the sofa, then lurching up. Gramary came into the kitchen and plopped into the chair across from Merkka. "We'll talk," she said. "Only thing to do is talk or sing until it stops bothering you."

How did Gramary, who had never been afraid of anything, know that? Merkka couldn't talk about the storm and how she felt, but maybe she would be able to tell Gramary about what Charlie Budge had done to the dog.

"Gramary," she began, "what if I saw someone we know doing something bad? A grown-up."

"Something bad?" said Gramary. "Like breaking the law?"

Merkka nodded, then shook her head. "I'm not sure."

"But you're sure that you saw it?"

"Yes," said Merkka. "No," she added quickly. "Pretty sure."

Gramary leaned back and considered. After a moment she said quietly, "I wouldn't want to go around accusing anyone of a bad thing unless it was clear as day to me—the someone and the deed."

Merkka took this in. It wasn't fair. How could it be clear as day when she could barely see what had actually happened off Charlie's boat?

"You want to tell me?" Gramary asked her.

Merkka stared at the table where a hot pan had seared its shape into the wood. She shook her head.

For a moment they sat in silence. A huge gust of wind rocked the house. The light blinked.

"Then we'll sing," said Gramary.

Gramary started with "Rocked in the Cradle of the Deep," not in her usual singing voice, but in a hushed way that lulled and softened the stormy feeling all around them. Merkka drew her feet up and hugged her knees. It was hard to keep her head from lolling right over on them.

"Get yourself to bed," Gramary said to her. "You won't do that dog any good fussing and worrying anymore tonight."

"I'm not tired," Merkka mumbled.

"If you're all dragged out and dopey tomorrow, you'll be no help at all to me."

"Tomorrow?" Merkka started awake. Gramary had her scheming look. She was planning something. "Tomorrow?"

"Shh!" Gramary warned. She nodded at Merkka.

Just knowing that they would do something about the dog tomorrow changed the way Merkka felt about going to bed. She told Gramary to keep the light on until she was all the way under the covers. Then she started up the stairs.

CHAPTER 5:

Jetsam

A long time ago when I was I don't know how old, I thought I saw Grampa in a tide pool. Gramary and Mrs. Cope had been talking about this and that. Then something came up about a boy that drowned in the quarry. They were going on about how awful it was, worse than anything, even Grampa. Dayle, they said. Worse than Dayle.

I'm sure I already knew that he had drowned, but that's my first memory of people talking about it in an everyday way. I hoped they'd say more about Grampa drowning, but they got to talk about Mrs. Cope's son, Forrest, and his family. It was boring, so I wandered off to wait for Gramary on the rocks beside the old pier. Pretty soon I was stirring up starfish in a tidal pool.

When you squat down and shut out everything else, you see a whole world in one of those pools. There are

*mountains and jungles in them, all wild and full of
prehistoric creatures like the kind you see in books
about dinosaurs. I was crouched right over that world,
practically in it, when all of a sudden there was this
face under the water, eyes wide open, mouth open, hair
spread out. Grampa. It was a little like the picture of
him when he was a sailor, only blurry and splotched.
For a second I thought he saw me. I didn't move. I
couldn't. Then it came to me: If he sees me, he can't be
drowned.*

*I stuck my hand in to pull him out. I couldn't touch
him, though. He went right through the rock bottom of
the pool.*

*"Grampa!" I screamed. I nearly lost my balance,
nearly fell in after him. I sat back and shut my eyes. I
could hear the gulls laughing all around me. I felt the
sun and the wind on the back of my neck. I smelled fir
trees and rotting sea urchins. And when I looked again,
I saw myself in that rock pool, my own face full of
ripples and creases like a cardboard box floating in the
water with the glue come off it.*

During the night the wind dropped and the rain began to fall.
Merkka woke in the dark to hear the drumming on the roof
and the pinging on the cars and the bus in the yard below. She
pulled the covers tight to her ears, but she could still hear that
rain, and she knew it was pelting the wreck and the dog and
every living thing that was not under some sort of cover. When
she finally fell asleep again, it was late. Or else early in the
morning. And when Mom yelled through the door that if she
wanted a ride to school she'd better get a move on, she only
buried herself in her bed and squeezed her eyes tight shut.

The next thing she knew, Dad stood over her. "I'm dropping your mother off at work," he said. "I'll drop you at school, too, if you hurry."

"Where are you going?" she mumbled.

"Better ask *when* I'm going. The answer is in five minutes."

"I'll walk," she said.

"It's pouring."

"I'll walk."

She heard him stop at Ben's bed, but he didn't say anything more. Sometimes when Ben was sleeping Dad just touched him very quietly.

A few minutes later Gramary came in. She whipped the covers off both the children, informed them that it was now or never, and threw winter socks at each of them because they'd be in their boots and she didn't want to hear a word about cold toes. "Dress your feet!" is the way she put it.

Merkka sat shivering on the edge of her bed. "I missed a ride with Dad," she said.

Gramary, who was yanking a heavy sweater over Ben's head, said, "Just as well. I'd only have fetched you out again, and that would've caused a ruckus at school."

"Are we going in the *Little Mary*?"

Gramary struggled with Ben, who was trying to wriggle out of the sleeves because his shirt was all bunched up inside them. "Not *Little Mary*," said Gramary. "We need something that handles speedy. We'll take Charlie's runabout."

Downstairs, after lukewarm cocoa and cold toast, they bundled into boots and foul-weather gear and trooped down to the harbor. It looked to Merkka as though every boat in Ledgeport was inside the breakwater. Out beyond, toward the Porcupines, Merkka saw black squall lines creasing the gray surface of the bay. Yet she could feel no wind here. It was very strange. And all around her the steely rain drilled holes through the slick surface of the water.

Gramary opened the door to the boat shed to see if Charlie

Budge was inside. "Tell him," she said to Ed Ingalls, "I'm taking the loan of his boat. Won't be long."

"I wouldn't go outside, Mary," Ed advised. "It'll be blowing for real before you know it."

Norm Gray said, "Wouldn't take them kids out neither. Wouldn't take myself out."

Gramary gave them a curt nod. "You tell Charlie if he shows up." She marched Ben and Merkka down the ramp.

When Gramary pulled the runabout alongside the float, Ben hesitated. "I wish we were going in Dad's boat," he said. "This one doesn't have a house."

Gramary gave him a considering look and sent him back up to wait in the boat shed. Then she beckoned Merkka aboard. As soon as they were free of the float, they zoomed out toward the breakwater. The rain made a terrific racket in the boat; the outboard whined. Merkka hunched down inside the hood of her jacket to keep as warm and dry as possible. She didn't raise her head until she heard Gramary slowing down. Then she looked around. They were just passing the monument now. The massive black hull of the wreck loomed before them in the falling tide.

Even on a sunny day the wreck gave Merkka the shivers. Some of the older kids climbed up on it once in a while; the bravest ones dove off it. But mostly people steered clear, because even when the tide was high you could lose your footing climbing up it and give yourself a nasty scrape.

As Gramary slowed and scanned the wreck, Merkka looked too. What if they couldn't find the dog? What if they gave up and it was there after all, trapped inside?

"There!" Gramary pointed.

It took a moment before Merkka realized that she was looking at the dog. It was huddled on a timber, its paws like hands gripping the side, its coat so black and spiky it looked oiled or tarred.

Gramary sidled up until she was just below the dog. But far

below. There was nothing to tie up to, so she called Merkka to the helm and told her to move the boat forward very slowly to keep from slipping back with the current. Merkka tried, but went too far. She had to circle around and get in position again. Gramary was ready with the boat hook as Merkka brought them underneath the dog.

"Too close," Gramary called. "Ease us off a little." She tried to dislodge the dog, which drew itself tighter and clung for dear life.

"It'll fall into the water," Merkka protested.

"Only way," Gramary answered. "We'll fish it out." Gramary grunted as she struck the timber just to one side of the dog. It shrank back from the hook, then swiveled, snapping at it. That made it slip. As it lost its perch, it clung for just a second, its forepaws like black hands splayed out against the slimy surface. Gramary jabbed the boat hook behind it. Merkka could hear the claws scraping the side of the hull as the dog plummeted.

"Don't move the boat!" Gramary shouted to Merkka.

"We're drifting," Merkka called back.

The black head surfaced right beside the wreck; the paws clawed for a toehold. Then the dog swam along and tried again. Everywhere it made contact with the hull, it seemed to start to climb out of the water before falling back. Merkka was sure that if they brought the boat any closer, the dog would be crushed against the wreck.

Gramary took over the helm again. She poked the boat in close, forcing the dog farther and farther along the hull. By now the dog scarcely drew itself up. It only turned toward the hull as if looking for a surface it could grip. Gramary told Merkka to steer for the wedge, to drive the boat right through.

"I'll hurt it!" Merkka sobbed, but she followed Gramary's directions, her eyes on the slicker-clad arm that pointed first one way, then another. Then suddenly the arm was gone. Most of Gramary was gone. Merkka ran forward to grab Gramary's legs. She held tight until the top part of Gramary reared up from the water clutching the soaked, ragged black thing that scarcely resembled a dog anymore. Only it was the other way around, Merkka realized. It was the dog that clutched Gramary, her hand firmly locked between its jaws.

The boat rocked so hard Merkka staggered. Through a blur of tears and rain she saw Gramary fling the dog down and tie it with pot warp. The dog lay in a cowering heap, its eye on Gramary, who squelched back to the helm and turned the boat away from the wreck. As soon as they were clear, she reached over the side to dunk her hand in the water. After a moment she brought it up. At first Merkka thought it looked all right, but then blood spots appeared. The blood spread all over Gramary's hand. Merkka screamed.

Gramary, steering with her good hand, told Merkka that if she didn't quiet down she'd scare the dog overboard. By the time they came around the end of the breakwater and the boat stopped rolling so badly, Merkka was able to stow the hook and the pot warp Gramary hadn't used.

By now the storm was bearing down on the harbor. Gramary wasted no time going in. When they reached the float, she gave Merkka the rope she'd tied on the dog and sent her up to the boat shed.

Merkka, head down against the rain, ran full tilt until she started up the ramp. Then she was stopped. The dog had flattened itself on the float at the foot of the ramp. Merkka stared at it through the downpour. It didn't look like something that could bite through skin and flesh; it was just something tossed up by the storm. But Merkka didn't dare reach down to it. She waited for Gramary to finish securing the boat.

When Gramary finally came pounding over, she took in the situation at a glance and scooped the dog up so fast it didn't have time to bite her again.

They burst in through the door of the boat shed. No one seemed to notice what Gramary was carrying until she lowered it to the floor. Ben ran over to it, but Gramary made him keep back. "It's scared," she said. "It doesn't know you."

Ed Ingalls looked it over. "Doesn't look like the dangerous critter Russell Leeward told us of. The way Russ put it, the dog was so vicious it ought to've drowned."

"It bit Gramary," Merkka informed him on a note of pride. Gramary hadn't been put off by any warning snarl.

"You'll have to have all them shots," Spike Breslaw remarked to Gramary. "In case the dog's got rabies."

Gramary said that was a bunch of nonsense, but she'd take a clean rag if anyone had such a thing. She'd wash her hand off good when she got home. "It's the dog wants care," she added, "not me."

They all looked down at the black lump at her feet.

"Black as a shag," said Ed Ingalls. "That wouldn't be the dog Charlie had out to the island, would it?"

"Charlie with a dog?" said Gramary.

"To clear off the sheep," Norm Gray put in. "If it is, it's a sorry sight now. The dog I recollect seeing had white on it and prick ears."

"'Course," said Spike, "Charlie'd be looking for it. Everyone knows there was a dog on the wreck. Three days."

Norm shook his head. "Charlie's gone. Visiting his sister down to Massachusetts."

Merkka saw the dark figure in the boat, saw him stooped down and then rising up to heave something overboard. She looked from Gramary to Ed Ingalls and the others. They were all nodding, agreeing that, to be sure, Charlie would've inquired if he'd lost a dog.

"Didn't tell me about it," snapped Gramary. "Not a thing about any dog."

"We just happened to see him go out that day," Norm told her. "He didn't want anyone to know."

Gramary muttered something about Charlie hiding things, and Merkka quickly changed the subject, asking if they could keep the dog.

Gramary didn't reply.

Ben said, "What will we call him?"

Gramary leaned over, tried to pull the dog to its feet, held it a moment, and watched it slump to the floor again. "It's a boy dog," she told him, "and if we don't get him home and put some food into him, we'll have to call him dead."

"That's not a name," Ben objected.

Gramary straightened. "You're right. How about Jet?"

Ben looked doubtful. "Like a plane?"

"Because he's jet black," said Ed. "That's the blackest you can get."

Gramary picked the dog up. It didn't even try to bite her this time. She carried it like a baby with its head over her shoulder. They detoured to Stan's Market. Merkka went in and asked Stan for a bag of dog food and they'd pay for it later. Gramary was already on her way down Water Street when Merkka came out of the store. By the time she reached home, lugging the dog food, the dog was in the kitchen circling and scratching at Gramary's old jacket that she'd spread out on the floor for him. Gramary said the jacket didn't owe her anything, not after twelve years. She poured warm water over the dry dog food and let the pot sit a moment. When she set it down, the dog drank all the warm liquid. After that, he lunged at the food, swallowing it in great, convulsive gulps. When he was finished, he trotted over to the other side of the kitchen and threw up.

"What's he doing?" cried Ben. "Is he going to die?"

The dog hung over the mess it had made, turned away, then turned back and ate it all up from the floor.

"Now Mom won't know about it," Ben said. "Now he's well again."

Merkka was already worried about what Mom would say. She tried to wipe the floor with paper towels, but she wasn't sure where the mess had been anymore. Everything was wet.

Gramary thought to take him out. She didn't bother with the rope. She just walked to the door and called to him. He slunk toward her, his tail between his legs and tight up against his skinny belly. "I'm not throwing you out," she told him. "Just do your business, and we can both get back in out of the rain." Then she shut the door, leaving Ben and Merkka in the kitchen.

After a while Ben said, "He's run away. Gramary can't find him. She should've used the rope."

Merkka imagined something worse. She pictured Charlie Budge driving fast the way he drove his boat. On his way here, because the men had told him over to Ingalls' that Gramary had his dog. Soon they would hear brakes squealing and the yelp of the dog. One time she'd heard that. They'd all heard it in school, heard it through the walls and the closed windows. And when they went out at recess, there was the dog, lying on its side. If Charlie's truck hit this dog, it wouldn't be an accident like that other one, because Charlie had already tried to kill him.

But nothing happened. Gramary and the dog returned, both of them more soaked than before, if that was possible. Gramary sent Merkka for bath towels. The dog stood for the rubbing, head down, bony shoulders and back swaying under Gramary's hands. When Gramary was finished, she plunked the dog down on the jacket. This time there was no digging, no circling. The dog stayed flopped over.

Ben peered down at him, but Gramary armed him away. "Never crowd an animal. They need space," she explained.

Merkka kept her distance, but she noted the rise and fall of the dog's rib cage. She also saw that the dog had white on his belly and legs. There was even white on his muzzle and the tip of his tail. The rain had cleaned off some of the wreck slime. The scrubbing had fluffed out the hair and revealed a pattern of white on the mostly black body.

Gramary opened a can of soup and heated it up. She considered sending Merkka to school for what remained of the day, then decided to let her stay home if she did another page in her workbook. The rain drummed and spattered all around them. The dog seemed to hear it from far off. It twitched and sighed and slept on.

When Dad came home, no one had time to tell him about the dog. As soon as he was inside, pulling off his slicker and hanging it on a hook, the dog was up with a bound and across the floor. Then he halted. His wagging tail slowed; his head turned slightly away.

"Spike and Ed think it might be Charlie's," Gramary told Dad.

Dad looked at the dog. "I didn't know Charlie got a dog. You call him?"

Gramary said, "He's gone to Gloucester."

Dad scootched down on his heels. The dog sidled up to him.

"Well," Gramary went on, "it's a man's dog. That's clear."

Dad rubbed the dog on the neck and chest, then rose. "Feed it?"

Gramary snorted. "What do you think? But it can have a little more now. It's been sleeping."

This time the dog chewed the food before swallowing it. Dad said he hoped they found the owner before the dog ate them out of house and home. Then he saw the crestfallen look on Ben's face and laughed. That meant, thought Merkka, that Dad might be willing to keep the dog if they couldn't find his owner. Thank goodness he had run at Dad with his tail wagging. Thank goodness Gramary didn't seem to blame the dog for her bitten hand.

CHAPTER 6:

Settling In

When I was little, I always drew our house with a peaked roof and the chimney going off crooked. Since I couldn't get the chimney straight, I concentrated on all the other important details. The windows had curtains and the yard had flowers and trees. Never mind if the flowers were as tall as the trees. They were there where they should be.

Sometimes I made a picture of my family inside the house. Mom and Dad and baby Ben and my grandmother in a longer skirt than Mom's because that was the way grandmothers are supposed to look. I really thought what I was drawing was true. And there would be a cat on the rug in front of the fireplace, even though we don't have rugs in our house or a fireplace and we've never had a cat. Or a dog. I always drew a dog beside the front door.

Ben began making pictures when he was even littler.
Everyone said he would be an artist. His pictures of our
home showed a house on a steep hill and part of it on
pilings over the water. There were no curtains in his
pictures, no cat on a rug in front of a fireplace, and no
dog next to the door. Outside, instead of trees and
flowers, he would draw a car chassis and truck parts
and boat gear and a weapons carrier and a school bus
with its side cut open. He wasn't as good at people as he
was at things, but he always showed Gramary wearing
overalls and holding a welding torch. Sometimes all you
saw of her was her helmet. In Ben's pictures she was
usually bigger than Mom and Dad, even though she is
short and sort of square. So Ben didn't get everything
perfect, even though he came pretty close. And from the
start, he knew how to set his chimney on a sloping roof
so that it stuck straight up to the sky.

There was no real trouble over the dog until Mom came home
and made Gramary unwrap the bandage on her hand. Then
there was an argument, the kind kids stay out of.

Mom said, "If it bit you, it'll bite Ben or Merkka. Or a neighbor. We're in enough trouble with the town without that happening."

Dad said, "We'll find out who owns it. Don't worry."

Gramary said, "The town's got nothing to do with this dog.
They left him to drown."

"Wait till it snaps at Mr. Sprague," Mom shot back.

Dad tried to calm her down. "Ma's been here a lot longer
than Harley Sprague and all those complainers up the hill that
think they've bought the whole town of Ledgeport."

"When the plant shuts down, they're all we'll have left here.

When you have to take whatever price the wholesalers offer, you'll be grateful for every customer up the hill. And you'll have to buy your bait somewhere else too."

Dad said he'd just been over to see Henry about the bait truck route; things would all work out. But Mom wasn't in a mood to be reassured. Sometimes she felt better after she had a chance to relax and put her feet up, but tonight she just fell asleep on the sofa, which was also Gramary's bed.

Dad and Gramary went on talking in the kitchen. Merkka couldn't help thinking about Lucy's house, with a room for every member of the family. She asked Dad whether they would have to move when the fish plant shut down.

Dad told her they wouldn't. "Mom's just upset about losing her job, because she makes good money there."

Ben flipped back the page of the pad he was drawing on. "What's bad money like?" he asked.

Dad and Gramary laughed. "No such thing," Gramary told him.

But Dad really answered him. "Mom wants us to have . . . more."

Ben looked around. "More money?"

"More to live with," Dad said. "Space. Maybe a home of our own."

"This is a home of our own, and now we have a dog for it," Ben said.

"This is your grandmother's home."

"And yours as well," put in Gramary.

"Only sometimes Mom feels crowded."

"Like Jet," said Ben.

Gramary nodded, but Dad warned that even if they gave the dog a name, he might not be here long enough to learn it.

Merkka asked if it was still all right to call him Jet now that the white parts were showing.

"Black wasn't what I had in mind," Gramary answered. "I was thinking of jetsam."

Both children knew what that meant, because Mrs. Cope called the junk they picked off the island shore flotsam and jetsam. Jet for jetsam, thought Merkka. She liked the sound of the name better than its meaning. But Ben was way ahead of her, his face screwed up with figuring. "Then we have to get another dog and call it Flotsam."

Gramary and Dad laughed again. They sounded as though they were getting used to the idea of a dog in the house.

When Merkka went to bed that night, she considered telling Ben about what Charlie had done, but something made her hold back. After all, Gramary and Ben had seen what she had seen, and yet neither of them seemed to suspect that the bundle Charlie threw overboard was Jet. Even if she could convince Ben, she doubted she could make Gramary believe such a thing about someone she'd known and worked with for years and years. If Ben were a little older, she could count on him not to blurt it out, but he wasn't good at keeping things to himself. Merkka needed time to work out how they could protect Jet. If he caused a fuss, Mom would probably insist on getting rid of him.

Merkka thought and thought. Then she said to Ben, "If it is Charlie's dog, he doesn't deserve to have it if he goes off and leaves it like that."

"Oh," said Ben. Then, with enthusiasm, "He doesn't deserve it. What if it belongs to someone else?"

"No one deserves it," Merkka retorted, "not if they deserted it." But she was worried about Charlie coming back and claiming the dog.

Tomorrow came, and the next day, and the day after that. Nothing happened to Jet except that Alan Greeley came to take a picture of him and Gramary for the *Muskeag News.*

Then at suppertime Dad informed them that Jet really was Charlie's dog. Charlie had bought him off Bobby Brackett, who was away at the university this year. Ever since Bob Senior had his back trouble and they cut back on their herd, there wasn't all that much work for the dog. "Paid a fair sum for it too," Dad added with a smile. "Seems Charlie wanted to keep it quiet, how Suzy Cope said when she left for Boston that whoever took the sheep off her island could keep all but ten she wants back next summer. They've been eating her fruit trees and garden, so she wanted them all off for now."

"Well," Gramary pointed out, "the sheep are still there. I expect we'll hear about it when Charlie gets back and needs help with them."

"How did Jet get on the wreck?" Ben asked.

"We'll hear about that too," Gramary told him.

"We ought to give the Bracketts a call," Mom said. "The dog should go back there."

"He's not theirs anymore," Merkka put in. "Bobby sold him." Then she added, "He's just getting used to us. And there's the newspaper coming out about Gramary saving him and all."

"We don't need the *News* calling attention to your grandmother right now," snapped Mom.

"It may make some people feel a bit more kindly toward her," Dad suggested.

Gramary pushed her chair back and stood up. Jet jumped to attention, his eyes on her. "You start playing their games," Gramary declared, "and they'll beat the pants off you."

"Really, Mary!" Mom retorted.

Gramary went on speaking to Dad. "This yard was good enough for you when you were growing up here, and for half the town. There was a time when I was the only one who could fix things good enough to keep them going. There's a few people around here with awfully short memories. They need reminding."

"You can't live on memories," Mom said to her. She wasn't shouting, but her words came out hard and tight. "Times change. You've got to change, too, or you'll be in trouble. We'll all be in trouble. They don't want this dump here anymore. They have all the welders they need now, not in plain sight of the best houses, but out behind the garages. All the trawlers have their own welders too. It's over, Mary. It's past." Mom's face was flushed. "People talk about it at work."

"Well, you won't have to listen to them when the plant shuts down. I wouldn't be surprised if some of them get to looking for a little work in their own backyards to keep them going."

Mom started to reply, then just shook her head.

"Beverly," said Dad. "Bev, Ma doesn't mean—"

"I'm not saying I want to see the plant shut down," Gramary went on. "I didn't mean to upset you, Bev. Let's drop it." She picked up some dishes and carried them to the sink. When she returned for more, she reached over Mom's shoulder. For just an instant Gramary's hand touched Mom's sleeve. "It's bad for you to worry so," Gramary said, her voice low.

After a moment Mom nodded. She leaned back and let her head rest against Gramary's ample front. Then, with a sigh, she said, "Anyway, there's not much I can do about it. Not much any of us can do." She sat up straight again and stared at the wall.

Dad spoke, too, his voice matching Mom's and Gramary's. Merkka wondered if they thought she wouldn't bother to listen. Of course, it worked just the other way around. When they shouted, Merkka tended to get out of their way. When their voices dropped like this, she sat very still to catch every word. Dad was telling them that the word at the wharf was that it was pressure from up the hill that was forcing the plant to close. The smell. There was a new law about it that cost too much to conform to. A no-win situation for the waterfront.

"I know." Mom nodded miserably.

Gramary ran water into the dishpan. "And what's the word on Charlie?" she asked. "Anyone know when he's coming back?"

Dad said not that he knew of. They all turned to look at Jet, who was lying on the floor behind Gramary. Without raising his head, his eyes registered their attention. His tail whacked twice.

CHAPTER 7:

Magic Words

You can get so used to some things that you stop noticing them. A lot of Gramary's scrap metal is like that for me. So are some of the funny things she makes for Ben and me and for Mrs. Cope. Ben has a toy weapons carrier put together from pot lids and blocks from broken pulleys and busted cleats. Every time something falls off, Gramary adds a new part. When she's not repairing it, Ben has it with him, but I hardly see it anymore, even when it's changed. For some reason, though, I never miss looking at the giant herring Gramary made for the fish plant years ago when it was a sardine cannery. Maybe because the herring is so big; maybe because it's so simple. She used two sleigh runners and set them bowed out for the body, and then she added parts from an old boat transom for the head. The cannery used it for a sign for years and

years, and it just stayed on because everyone expected
it to be there. I don't know why it always surprises me.
It's like a magic trick. I can recognize the sleigh runners
still. Yet if I blink once, there's just that herring in their
place.

Reports about the plant closing took up most of the front page
of the *Muskeag News*. Merkka found the picture of Jet and
Gramary at the bottom of page three, along with an article
crediting Mrs. Mary Weird of Water Street in Ledgeport with
rescuing a black mongrel dog moments before last week's
storm swept in with tides running four feet above normal.
Without Mrs. Weird's prompt action, the sea would surely have
taken the dog.

"Weird!" cried Merkka. "Mary Weird! I'll never go to school
again!"

"If it's a mistake," Dad informed her, "you can ask them to
print a correction."

"Will they do that? Will you make them?"

"Or maybe they wrote it that way on purpose." He was actually grinning.

Gramary came in the side door with Jet at her heels. "I've
got me a second bus," she told Dad. "Coming tomorrow."

"Isn't that likely to provoke one or two people up the hill?"

Gramary shrugged. "Soon as I've got the two buses set up,
they'll be a workshop and they won't bother anyone. Norman
bought this one off the regional school for the engine. He knew
I could use the body."

There was no point speaking to Gramary about the misprint
in the paper. Being called Mary Weird wouldn't bother her at
all.

At school no one had read the article about the dog yet, so
Merkka was able to breathe easily. But she thought to ask Miss
Guarino what could be done if a newspaper printed something

about you that wasn't true. Miss Guarino wrote a few words on the blackboard: *retract* was one of them; *slander* was another. When she began to talk about freedom of the press, Merkka stopped listening.

That afternoon she found a note on the kitchen table telling her that Gramary and Ben were working on the new old bus at Norm Gray's. So when the phone rang, Merkka figured it wouldn't be Gramary. Maybe it was Joan Greeley calling to say how sorry she was that the *Muskeag News* had slandered the Weir family.

"Hello!" Merkka shouted into the telephone.

"Where's Charlie Budge?" demanded a crisp, dry voice, which Merkka recognized at once as Mrs. Cope's. "He won't answer his phone."

"He's not there," Merkka said. "He's away."

"How did that dog get on the wreck?"

Merkka was struck dumb. Mrs. Cope was calling all the way from Boston about the dog. "Gramary's not here," Merkka said lamely.

"Well, tell her to get that dog out on the island and round up the sheep. She can have the lot of them. I told Charlie. I told him whoever gets the sheep off Grace Island can have all but ten."

"How do you know about the dog?" Merkka asked.

"The newspaper, of course. All my mail's forwarded here. I don't want Charlie trying again. He's bound to lose the dog. You tell Mary to do it for me."

"Yes, all right, I'll tell her."

"I warned him," Mrs. Cope went on. "I saw how that dog cowered when he yelled at it. 'Ask him nicely,' I said. But then what do I know about sheep dogs? Charlie doesn't like me interfering. Well, he's had his chance. Mary can do it. Tell her I'm counting on her to get the job done." There was a click. Mrs. Cope had hung up.

But when Merkka delivered Mrs. Cope's message that night,

Gramary shrugged it off. "I don't know what makes her think I can do it if Charlie couldn't."

"He yelled," Merkka supplied.

"They always yell. Last sheep drive I recollect, we had half a dozen people running and yelling and only one that knew the right commands for the dog."

"Are we going to have all the Grace Island sheep?" asked Ben.

Mom pressed her hands to her eyes. She didn't even try to answer.

Dad said, "If Gramary can get the sheep, she'll sell them and make a little money." He turned to her. "You going to try?"

"I don't know. I can't think about it till the bus gets here. I can't think of anything else."

"Me too," said Ben.

Mom spoke from behind her spread fingers. "You'll have plenty more to think about when Harley Sprague sees what you're dragging down here."

The arrival of the bus was the sort of event that draws every kind of onlooker. If Mr. Sprague didn't know about the bus as it inched down the steep slope from Water Street and across the boat railway to Gramary's yard, just about everyone else did. Bob Brackett on his tractor hauled the bus with his front-end loader filled with stone to offset the weight he towed. Spike Breslaw recalled the time he had to drag out the beached whale. "A load behind like that swings you like a tail wagging a dog." Alan Greeley, his camera at the ready, kept running in front of the tractor to get a shot of the oncoming procession.

Bob Brackett never said a word to him. He just drove on, grinding everything small enough to be run over by his enormous rear wheels. Turns were tough. Once the bus got to rocking so badly Norm Gray had to shout to Bob Brackett to back up. Norm set a couple of planks across debris from an old boat cradle half sunk in the gravel. Bob Brackett managed to complete the turn.

Lucy Starobin, who was standing with Merkka, said, "I bet your grandmother will get her name in the paper again."

Merkka said, "If she was my other grandmother, she wouldn't have our name and no one would have to know she's mine."

"And then you wouldn't be famous," Lucy pointed out.

Merkka didn't bother to explain how she felt about that kind of fame.

Bob Brackett backed and filled to position the bus just where Gramary wanted it alongside the other one. Merkka and Lucy helped Ben hold onto Jet, who kept trying to hurl himself toward the tractor. As soon as the bus was set and leveled on concrete blocks and the chain unhitched, they let the dog go. Merkka watched his frantic leaps. She ran after him and shouted up to Mr. Brackett, "He's glad to see you."

"Expect so," Mr. Brackett answered. "There, Toby," he said. "Right there."

Jet sank down on his belly, his feet straight ahead. He looked ready to spring up again, but he didn't move.

Merkka was amazed. Just those few words, and all that jumping stopped. Maybe Mr. Brackett didn't know what had happened to Jet, or Toby. She started to tell him, but there was too much going on all around them, chains dragging, the tractor roaring, people crowded around someone jacking up the front end of the bus. Merkka stepped back and tried to make Jet come with her. He was deaf to her.

At the top of her lungs she shouted up to Mr. Brackett. "If I call him Toby, will he do what I say?"

"It's not the name," Mr. Brackett told her. "It's the right words. That'll do," he said to Jet, and the dog got up. "You tell him," Mr. Brackett said to Merkka. "He'll mind. It's only me being here that's got him confused."

"What are the right words?" she called up to him. "What do I say if I want him to get the sheep?"

"I expect it's the same as for cows, which is all he's ever

done for me. I suppose he'll fetch anything. I wouldn't doubt
he'd round up a school of herring if you ask him to."

"What would you tell him?"

"To bring in the herring?" Mr. Brackett was laughing now.
He swept his right arm wide. "I'd say, 'Away!' And if I wanted
him to go that way," he added, making a sweep with his left
arm, "I'd tell him to 'Come by.' That's how Bobby trained him.
Most dogs, you just tell them to get the cows, and they do. But
if you say, 'Get 'em!' to Toby, he'll go at them hard. Bobby
learned off the 4-H leader, so that's what Toby understands."

Merkka thought of the sheep scattered over Grace Island.
Whenever she went near them they'd run straight for the
woods. "What other words?" she asked.

"'Walk up.' That means come straight on to your cows."

Jet was standing erect, his head cocked with each command.
"See," said Mr. Brackett, "he's too smart to go running off
here. No cows, no herring. He's trying to figure it out. Now
you better catch ahold on him so he won't follow me home.
And when he's all done, tell him, 'That'll do!'"

"That will do?"

Mr. Brackett nodded. "That's what shuts him down. The
brake words, 'That'll do.'"

Merkka recited the words to herself: away; come by; walk
up; that'll do. She grabbed Jet's collar and started to haul him
back from the tractor.

"Watch out for 'Lay down!' though," Mr. Brackett called
down to her.

"Why?" she shouted.

"If he's out there fishing herring for you and you tell him to
lay down, he'll drown." Laughing, Mr. Brackett pulled away
from the yard and began the long climb up to Water Street and
on out to Quarry Road.

Merkka decided that if Jet rounded up all those wild sheep,
she would say something more to him. "Good boy," she prac-
ticed out loud. "Good Jet."

Feeling the whack of his tail against her side, she told him softly, "That'll do." He looked out toward the road. He seemed to yearn to be off after Bob Brackett. "Good boy," she said again. "That'll do." She could feel him listen to her. She let go of his collar and watched him walk slowly toward the outside stairs. He sank down, his muzzle between his paws.

She realized with a thrill of excitement that the words had worked like magic. They could work out on Grace Island too. Jet would gather up those pesky sheep that were eating Mrs. Cope's flowers and vegetables. It would be done before Charlie Budge came back to Ledgeport, and then there would be no reason for him to take Jet away from her.

CHAPTER 8:

Grown-up Talk

Families talk in different ways. In our house, Dad might say, "Lost a couple of traps today. Something at those lines." Gramary might answer, "That old pot warp's rotten." Mom usually goes off in another direction. "They may be taking herring off the Grand Manan seiners next month. To fill out." Generally Gramary or Dad will answer her. "That's where all our herring went. Canada." But often Mom changes the subject again. "Lorraine's starting that drinking. On the job too." "Poor thing," Gramary might say, and Ben would ask, "Why is she poor?" Mom always tells him, "Never mind."

I wonder why she starts talking about Lorraine at the plant if she doesn't want Ben to pay attention.

In Lucy's family they mostly talk at the same time, which gives them a chance to say more. But it's harder to listen to.

I used to think that what people said was what they were thinking about. Of course, I knew grown-ups had lots of secrets, all those things they tell us we'll understand when we're older. But sometimes I wish they would come right out and say what's on their minds.

It was hard to get Gramary to consider the Grace Island sheep. She kept walking around her new bus and jotting down angles and lines with her stubby pencil on a piece of wood. After a while she'd throw the wood scrap away and pick up another and start over. She sang, "Shall We Gather at the River." Then she sang, "Lord! Lord! Lord! You Sure Been Good to Me!" She made Merkka hold the end of the tape measure, first one place, then another. Ben wanted to hold it, too, but after a while his hand would slide down. So Merkka held the tape firmly and reminded Gramary about Mrs. Cope's orders.

The afternoon after the bus arrived, Mr. Leeward came to see Dad. Gramary was out writing measurements on the bus with indelible marker. Ben was fooling around in the Hudson, making race car noises. He stood at the wheel because the front seat was in the living room across from the sofa. Mom wasn't home yet when Mr. Leeward showed up, but Dad, just back from lobster fishing, was pulling off his boots.

"How's it going?" Mr. Leeward began.

"Thinning," Dad answered. "Inside's all fished out."

"Lobsters still shedding?" said Mr. Leeward.

Dad shook his head. "Been going on like this awhile. It's the scallopers dragging the bottom like they do."

"What can you do?" Mr. Leeward told him. "You go dragging too. You got to keep up with the times, one way or another."

Dad looked at Mr. Leeward. "Is that what you're here for, Russell? To advise me to keep abreast of the times?"

Mr. Leeward leaned on the kitchen table. When he pulled

back, Merkka heard the sticky sound of his hands coming off something left from breakfast. He said, "I'm here for . . . all of us."

"You mean town business?"

Mr. Leeward nodded. "In a way, yes. You see, Sam, a lot of people are worried about what's going to happen when the plant shuts down for good. It'll be hard times for a lot of us."

"Us?" Dad looked across the table at Mr. Leeward in his summer suit and clean shoes. Mr. Leeward had a modern office right on the town green with a white and gold real estate sign out front. He was friendly with all the newest people from away because he had helped them buy their summer homes. He knew the longtime summer people and the locals because his dad had been a fisherman and a boat builder. Dad said, "Seems to me, Russell, you're not doing too bad these days."

Mr. Leeward straightened. "I'm not doing bad for myself, but I'm doing all right, too, for people that need to sell a little land and make some money."

Dad didn't speak, but the look on his face made Merkka pay close attention.

"This property," Mr. Leeward went on, "you sell it, and you can buy any house in town and a new lobster boat, and still have money for the bank."

Dad shook his head.

"Now listen, Sam. The future of Ledgeport is in summer people. That means keeping it looking like what they want to spend their holidays in. It's our only hope. Hear what I'm saying, Sam?"

Dad said, "I hear."

"Everyone's complaining about this mess down here. The Harbor View Inn, they're ready to go to court over your mother's junkyard."

"It's not a junkyard," Dad said. "It's a workyard like Ed's boatyard and the machine shop and—"

"It's what it looks like and where it is," Mr. Leeward told

him. "Ida Billings can't put guests in her back rooms because of what they'd see. Harley Sprague says his garden outlook is ruined. And now there's another bus."

"There's no law against a bus. Ma's using it."

"She can't. It won't run. It was dragged here."

"She's converting it into a shop. That'll put some of the stuff that's out there under cover."

"Sam, between you and I, it looks like hell." Mr. Leeward's voice dropped. "Don't you see? This is your chance to get out at a good price. And I happen to know Bev would like that. Her and Ruth talk. Think about it, Sam. A nice home, maybe a patio and even a pool for the kids."

Dad waved toward the harbor. "They've got the whole Gulf of Maine to swim in."

"You know what I mean. A patio and a barbecue and a table with an umbrella."

Dad shoved back his chair and stood up. "Yes, well, it's not up to Bev and it's not up to me. All of this is Ma's except the bait shack, and I doubt that's deeded to me as yet."

"But you could talk to your mother. You could convince her that this is a good time to sell."

"I expect she knows that. I expect she knows it'll stay good and get better."

Mr. Leeward started to speak, then clamped his mouth shut.

Dad eased him toward the door. "Why don't you put it to her yourself?"

"Well, to tell you the truth, I thought you'd be more, well . . . Seems like there's never any time to sit around like our folks did, like Ed and Charlie and some of them. Maybe one day I'll get back to it. Maybe I'll hire on as stern man for you, Sam." Mr. Leeward laughed. "Throw away my tie and dig out the old seaboots." He laughed some more, but as soon as the screen door closed behind him, the laughter stopped.

"Is Russell Leeward going to work for you?" Merkka asked.

"I wouldn't bet on it," Dad told her.

Merkka went to stand beside him at the window. She could feel a chuckle coming up from deep inside him. He was watching Mr. Leeward pause beside the old boat railway. Gramary, a crowbar in her hand, came around from behind the buses. When she caught sight of Russell Leeward, she nodded briefly before climbing inside the new bus. Mr. Leeward stood a moment longer, took a step toward Gramary, then turned back. He walked briskly up the pitted road, stepping over timbers and brushing his coat sleeve where something ugly must have stuck to it.

After that the questions roiled up in Merkka like herring in a net. The questions had nowhere to go, so they just squirmed and flopped and smothered one another.

Dad was thoughtful. Mom was tight-lipped and tired. Gramary, aglow with pleasure, could hardly be drawn away from the buses for supper.

When they went up to bed, Merkka couldn't contain herself anymore. She told Ben they might be moving. She didn't mean to tell him. She only wanted to hear the idea spoken out loud.

"Where will I sleep?" Ben wanted to know.

"In your own room. Like Jay Starobin." Merkka pictured a room like Lucy's for herself, except that the walls would be lavender and there would be plastic violets on the bureau. Mrs. Leeward had plastic violets in her bathroom with shower curtains to match.

Ben said, "I don't want to sleep alone."

"Yes, you do," Merkka told him. "You'll love it."

"I'm going to ask Mom," he threatened.

Merkka said quickly, "You can have Jet to sleep with."

"Did Mom say so?"

"Mom doesn't know about it yet, so don't say anything. It's a surprise."

"Who does know?" Ben asked her.

"I can't tell you, because it's a secret," she explained. She waited tensely, wishing she had never started this. At last she heard the slow, snuffly sound of him sleeping.

CHAPTER 9:
Gathering

*At first having Jet was a little like having part of my
house picture come true. I couldn't help thinking that if
Mom could stand a dog, maybe we could get a cat too.
We were coming closer to my idea of a normal home.*

*But when I found out that certain words really
worked with Jet, and when he'd stick his nose in my
hand—not for food, but just to be close—there was no
picture or idea, only Jet himself. That meant that he
was my dog, or at least partly mine. I think he knew
that too.*

In the morning Dad was gone and Gramary was already out
with her buses when Merkka came downstairs. Mom put her
fingers to her lips. She liked to let Ben sleep late so she could
get off to work without complications. Gramary would get
Ben's breakfast when he woke up.

"What's a patio?" Merkka asked.

Mom, making a list, didn't answer right away. Finally she looked at Merkka. "A patio? It's like a terrace, a place to sit outside. Why?"

"I just wondered."

Mom stared at her list.

Suddenly Merkka blurted, "Could we have one?"

Mom laughed. "What, here? In the shade of those buses?"

Merkka guessed she had made Mom mad at her. She stirred her cornflakes until they were soggy.

Ben appeared in his pajamas.

"Up already?" Mom exclaimed.

"I didn't want to be alone," he mumbled. "Merkka said I can have Jet with me in the new house, so can I have him now?"

"What new house?" Mom demanded. She turned to Merkka. "What's going on?"

"Nothing," Merkka said. "Mr. Leeward was here yesterday talking to Dad about selling this place and buying a new house. So I thought—"

"No one mentioned it to me."

"Gramary doesn't know either," Merkka supplied.

"Oh." Mom slipped on her sweater. "We'll walk together. You can tell me more." She poured Cheerios into a bowl and set it in front of Ben. "After breakfast go out to Gramary," she told him. "Don't speak about this. You understand?"

Ben nodded, but Merkka could tell he didn't understand at all. "What can I talk about then?" he asked as Merkka scooped up the lunch bag Dad always made up for her before he left at dawn.

"Anything else," said Mom from the door. "And get your clothes on."

"Sheep," Merkka shouted to him as she left. "Talk to her about getting those sheep off Grace Island. Tell her I know the magic words to make Jet round them up."

Mom said, "You think that dog'll listen if you say please?"

Merkka nodded.

"You better not bring any sheep here unless you're planning to put them inside Mary's new bus," Mom told her.

"That's a good idea," declared Ben, milk dribbling down his chin.

"It is not. Wipe your mouth. It's a joke. The bus is not a barn. It's a bus, an eyesore. It's going to make everyone hate us." She started up Water Street. Merkka supposed that Mom had forgotten they were going to walk together, but then she slowed and waited for Merkka to catch up.

"Now what's all this about moving?" Mom asked.

Merkka tried to think back to yesterday with Mr. Leeward. It was hard to sort out what she had heard from what she had added on when she was lying in bed afterward decorating her own room. "I'm not sure," she said. They were at the corner of Water Street and Mill Street. Mom had to go on past the town wharf; Merkka had to turn up toward the green.

Lucy was waiting for her outside of school; she started right off talking about someone's birthday. Merkka scarcely listened. Her thoughts were a jumble of lavender walls and patios.

Ben and Gramary met her after school. The *Little Mary* was ready, Jet already tied inside it, lest he take it into his head to jump out.

"You never know what'll spook a dog," Gramary remarked as she started up the engine.

Now that they were under way, Merkka didn't feel so sure about making Jet work. "Do you know the words too?" she asked Gramary.

Gramary shook her head. "You'll have to say them. Then the sheep'll be yours too."

"Mine?" Merkka had never pictured sheep in her dream house.

As they drew near to Grace Island, Gramary shut down the throttle. The engine clanked and then stalled. Gramary said softly, "Look! There they are." Twenty or more sheep grazed on the bald point beyond the trees. Gramary looked at Jet, who was on his feet, his tail low and his ears high.

"Funny," she mused. "Charlie always brings the sheep down to the pens. Then it's an awful chore dragging them to the boat."

Merkka knew that the pens that were used at shearing and for sorting were all the way over on the other side of the island. "What are we going to do?" she asked.

Gramary started up the engine. They chugged in toward a line of pot buoys below the wooded shoreline. "We're going to drop you and Jet off here," Gramary told her. "You keep ahold on his rope. I'm going around till I'm just short of the point. We'll be across from each other."

"Where am I going?" Ben wanted to know.

"With me," Gramary told him. "You'll be my sheep dog." She studied the waterline on the rocks. "We'll have to wait, though." She told Merkka where to go. Everything depended on keeping the sheep from seeing her or the dog. "When I blow the horn, you send him toward me, and I'll make a lot of noise so they run away from me. That'll start them going toward you. They'll head for the woods if they can. Don't let them."

Merkka pictured all the sheep running straight at her. They'd knock her down.

"You tell the dog," Gramary went on. "Say the words to make him push them out to the point. Then you go along after them."

Merkka's heart pounded. What if she forgot the words?

"I can bring the boat in close on the other side," Gramary was saying. "You just drive them out on that spit."

"Into the water?"

"Right over the mussel bed and onto the islet." Gramary pointed to the low mound of green that tipped the end of the point. When the tide was full, it stood by itself like a tiny island.

As soon as Gramary eased the boat in among the rocks, Merkka clambered over and called to Jet. He landed on rockweed and slid backward into the water. Merkka waited until he had scrambled up, and then she worked her way shoreward with Jet slithering after her. Meanwhile Gramary headed out and around the island away from the sheep.

Once Merkka had gained the solid shore, she rested a moment on the scratchy ground at the base of a fir tree. It smelled of summer still, needles and leaf mold, raspberries and sun. Yet the bunchberry leaves had already turned russet. Merkka felt as though she were sitting between the seasons, with summer on one side and fall on the other.

Jet leaned his wet body against Merkka's pulled-up legs. She felt little tremors shake him. That made her feel sorry for him and glad all at the same time. "You're all right now," she whispered. "We'll never leave you to drown." He looked out toward the point. His nose twitched.

Starting along the island, she found it hard to keep close to the trees because the branches came so low. But Gramary said that was the way to stay out of sight. So Merkka crouched and sometimes went on her hands and knees. All the while she kept telling Jet to stay beside her. He seemed to understand.

Suddenly everything brightened. There ahead of her the long grass and raspberry canes lay in curving swaths. When she stood up, she could see the sheep grazing on the downward slope. Beyond them the mussel bed darkened the glittering shallows. On the islet gulls quarreled, rising suddenly and circling. Good, thought Merkka. With all the clamor, the sheep would hear nothing else.

Now Merkka could see the *Little Mary* moving toward the point. Ben waved, and Merkka waved back. She started down the slope, Jet at her side. She dreaded the moment when she would have to send him away from her.

Gramary blew a blast on the old tin horn. Merkka grabbed Jet around the neck and pointed with her left hand. "By," she ordered. "Good boy. By."

He took off so fast she nearly called him back. How could she control him once he was gone? He disappeared among the trees, then emerged on high ground. "There!" she called to him. "Right there, Jet!" She held her breath, waiting to see if he heard and obeyed. She couldn't find him. She had to climb uphill some more. There he was again, midway between the shores of the neck and the point. Now what? Magic words. "Walk up," she called softly. "Walk up," she repeated, raising her voice.

Jet crouched, his head so low that only his ears pricked above the grass. Merkka kept forgetting to look where she was going. When she stumbled, the sheep heard the stones that clattered down to the water. As if on signal, all the sheep bunched up. They were looking at Merkka, though, not at Jet. She didn't know what to say to him. She didn't know what to do.

Gramary broke the deadlock by blowing the horn again and waving her arms. The sheep swung around and bolted, skittering over rocks and onto the soft turf above.

"Walk up!" Merkka shouted to Jet. "Stop them." That wasn't one of the words she'd learned, but she couldn't think of any others.

Jet showed himself to the sheep. They swerved, trying to duck toward the woods. He blocked their escape. They bounded the other way, and he was there too. Each time they found themselves face to face with the dog, they backed a little more toward the point.

Merkka kept to her side and tried to keep up with Jet and the sheep. Down in the water, coming slowly closer, the *Little Mary* nudged along the mussel bed. All of a sudden a few of the sheep turned and dashed out on the narrow spit and through the shallows to the islet. The others followed like sand running through an open hand.

Merkka had to shout to keep Jet from tearing after them. "That'll do!" she yelled at the top of her lungs, but it was Gramary's command that reached him and made him flatten himself in the water, holding the flock that huddled on the islet.

They had to wait for the tide to rise to get the boat in close enough. Lambs blatted and gulls circled furiously overhead. Finally Gramary called to Merkka and told her to try wading out. Her jeans were like wicks soaking up the cold water; she could hardly bend her knees. As she approached, the nearest sheep turned its wild yellow eyes on her. Meanwhile, Gramary was edging the boat in, stern first, on the other side. Then something happened that startled the sheep over there. They surged toward Merkka, and the staring one slipped down into the water.

Merkka called Jet, who swam toward the sheep and forced her back up onto the islet.

"All right," Gramary shouted from the other side. "We have two tied in here. Time to make the rest join their friends."

Merkka was out of words, magic or otherwise. She swept her arms at the sheep and let Jet come in really close at them. "Good boy," she gasped, hoping he would understand. It seemed for a while as if nothing was happening. Then she realized they were making headway. She and Jet were on the crown of the islet, and the sheep were following one another right into the lobster boat. When there were only four left, Gramary waded around to prod them along. She had to grab the last and drag it over the stern. It landed on the backs of others. After a little jostling, the packed sheep made room for it.

"There!" said Gramary on a note of satisfaction. "Twenty-two is what I count. How do you like that?"

Merkka liked it fine. So did Jet, who panted happily and leaned against Merkka while they waited for the tide to rise some more and lift the boat free.

CHAPTER 10:

Spelling Sheep

When I mention magic words, that doesn't mean I really think they have some special power. Still some words do kind of make things different. Only I can't figure whether it's the words themselves or the person speaking them.

Gramary brought the *Little Mary* to the float, stern first, so that Merkka and Jet could get out and block the ramp. Then Gramary tied up alongside and hauled one of the sheep over onto the float. Just the way they had gone into the boat, all the sheep but the two that were tied followed the first one over the side. The float rocked under the shifting lot of them. Gramary squeezed through and around Merkka. She said she was going to look for a truck with stakesides. All Merkka had to do was sit with Jet at the bottom of the ramp and keep the sheep from escaping.

A voice from above spoke to Merkka. "Mrs. Cope's sheep, ain't they?"

She looked up at Spike Breslaw. "I think they're mine now."

Spike leaned on the rail. "Looks like a fair lot of sheep to own all to once."

Merkka nodded proudly. She stood up to appear more in command. At her sudden move, all the sheep lurched. The float rocked some more.

Norm Gray shouted over the water to Spike. "What's going on. Can I gas up?"

"Traffic jam here," Spike called to him. "Better come around back." To Merkka he said, "Every customer Ed loses will cost you."

She knew he was teasing, but she wished Gramary would hurry up and come back. Everyone knew that Norm's old dragger had first rights at the float, since he could only make it around back when the tide was full.

She tried to keep an eye out for Gramary, but it was Charlie Budge who appeared next. Even though he wasn't a big man, he seemed to loom over Merkka.

"Cripes!" Charlie declared. Then he whistled. "What did Mary do? Cast a spell on them sheep?"

Merkka said, "She just backed the boat up to them and they were glad to get in."

"Cripes!" Charlie remarked to Spike and Norm, who joined him at the rail. "Those sheep are never glad to get in anywheres. Only out. It must've taken some powerful convincing. How many people did Mary have out there?"

Merkka answered him. "Just my brother and me and the dog."

"The dog!" exclaimed Charlie, who hadn't yet caught sight of Jet at the base of the ramp. "You found my dog?"

"He's not yours," Merkka retorted.

"If you found him on the island, he is."

"No," Spike told him. "That dog was on the wreck. Stuck there nearly three days."

Charlie leaned way over until he could see Jet at Merkka's

feet. "How did he get all the way here from Grace Island? That's one hell of a swim."

"You left him on Grace Island?"

Charlie shrugged. "Come to think of it, I don't really know. I had him out there with me a couple of days trying to get the sheep penned. We weren't communicating too good, him and me. By the time I quit, I was some fed up with him, and I guess he knew it." Charlie shook his head. "Never even noticed he'd taken off till I was nearly home. Then when I saw he wasn't in the boat, I figured he'd gotten out while I was stowing gear down to Mrs. Cope's float. As soon as I saw he was gone, I started to go back for him. Only it was getting dark, too late. I knew he'd be all right on the island. I'd left a bag of dog food he could get at. Probably catch himself a few rabbits too."

A good story, thought Merkka. Charlie Budge had had plenty of time to rehearse it.

Spike said, "Well, it looks like Merkka and Mary get the sheep."

Charlie didn't answer right away. Then he said, "But the dog belongs to me. Even though he turned out no good for what I got him for."

"He was fine!" Merkka blurted. "You just didn't know the magic words." As soon as she spoke, she realized her mistake. As long as Charlie Budge believed the dog was worthless, he might let him go.

"There you are," Charlie was saying to Norm and Spike. "Didn't I say so? Them Weirs and their spells."

Ed nodded. "That's right. Mary gets it from her old man. Reggie can tell you all about old Benjamin Weir up to the armpits at low tide fixing his weir. Wouldn't allow no alders, only birch trees. And always ahead of the full moon. Reggie spent one of those nights with him, Benjamin setting out there so still, never even slapping a mosquito. Them fish come like the tide to the moon, straight in. And him with his eyes near shut, his net cast, luring them. Those days one full weir could set you up for the year. Good days."

"So how about letting me in on some of those magic words," Charlie called down to Merkka.

"They're not real magic," she said. Maybe if she didn't make him mad he would leave Jet where he was. "It's not a real spell. It's just that Gramary can do things."

"We know," they all said together.

"And I know," Charlie added, "she must've spelled all them sheep to make them so agreeable. Here she is. We can ask her direct."

"Charlie," Gramary said, just as if she were picking up a conversation they had begun a little while ago, "did you have a place all set for these sheep ashore?"

Charlie grinned at her. "That field back of the barn where Bob sometimes keeps his dry cows. What's it worth to you, Mary, now that these sheep are yours?"

"Merkka's," she said.

While they were talking, a beautiful blue sloop with gleaming hardware headed into the wind and struck its white sails. The skipper called over to find out where to tie up for an hour or so and if there might be a spare mooring for overnight.

Ed told him to lay alongside the dragger, and Norm went down the ladder to hang out a tire fender.

"How long you using my float?" Ed asked Gramary.

Gramary answered that Bob Brackett was on his way as soon as he'd put the stakesides on his flatbed truck. Merkka sat down again, Jet between her knees. She knew what she would do now. She would trade some of her sheep, which were really hers, for the dog, which might really be Charlie's. She would wait for the right moment, make the offer, and add however many sheep it took to clinch the deal.

By the time the truck backed up to the wharf and sheets of plywood and rowboats tipped on their sides were lined up to make a chute, there was a small crowd assembled. Even Alan

Greeley showed up. He kept telling everyone to step aside so he could get a good picture of the dog driving the sheep up the ramp, but no one moved for him. Russell Leeward pushed through without asking, because he was harbormaster. He objected to the sheep; the manure would discourage yachts from coming into Ledgeport and give the town a bad reputation. But when the people off the blue sloop helped extend the chute by making themselves part of it, Mr. Leeward changed his tune and informed Joan Greeley that this kind of activity was steeped in tradition. He had Alan Greeley snap a picture of him with one hand on the stakeside of the truck and a sheep face just showing through.

Once the sheep were safely unloaded into the field beyond Charlie Budge's barn, Gramary and Charlie worked out an arrangement for keeping them.

Ben asked Merkka if she would let him have one of his own.

She thought a moment. "I will," she finally told him, "if you ask Charlie whether he wants to keep a dog that won't mind him."

"Why don't you ask him yourself?"

"I don't want to talk to him," she said.

When Ben looked doubtful, she added quickly, "Which sheep do you want? You have to pick one out."

"A little one," Ben said. He pointed to a lamb with a speckled face and a topknot of wool between its ears. "That one."

There were two or three other lambs so much like it Merkka wasn't sure she would be able to single it out later on. Never mind. Leave that to Ben. "Okay. What will you name it?"

"Grace," he said. "Because it comes from Grace Island."

"It might be a boy."

"I don't care. It's Grace."

"Well, don't forget what you have to ask Charlie," Merkka reminded him.

Later that night when they were in bed and Ben was drifting

off to sleep, Merkka prodded him with an insistent voice until he woke up enough to report to her.

"He doesn't care," Ben said. "We can feed Jet and stuff, just so's he's around when Charlie needs him."

Merkka heaved a great sigh. It felt good to let that worry slip into the darkness. Ten sheep for Mrs. Cope and one for Ben. That left eleven sheep and one black-and-white sheepdog that could make them go wherever you said. It was more than Merkka could have hoped for, Charlie Budge giving up Jet without even asking for a single sheep in exchange. She supposed Gramary had something to do with Charlie's decision, but Merkka couldn't be sure. Couldn't be sure, either, that Charlie Budge wouldn't change his mind later on.

If only Gramary had seen what Merkka had seen the night Charlie Budge tossed that bundle into the water. If Gramary knew what Charlie had done, she would never let him take Jet back, not ever.

CHAPTER 11:

Something for Everyone

I remember one day when Ben was a baby asleep with his head in the shade so the sun wouldn't bother him. I was watching Gramary fix something for Spike Breslaw. She made me turn my back to her. I thought that was because the magic would be spoiled if I looked while she was making it work. Now Ben was never like that. Right from the start he seemed to know all about welding. Only not when he was a baby with his head in the shade of Dad's bait shack.

Gramary was so busy she almost forgot us. Finally I asked if I could look, and she said yes. And I turned around. She'd cut a piece of shiny metal off the thing she was fixing. She picked up that piece and pulled it one way and then another the way you do folded paper. It became a sea gull. She put on her eye shield and made me turn from the sparks again, but only for a moment.

*When I was allowed to look, the gull had legs and a
beak; it hung from a wire attached to a little pole. She
clamped the pole to the door of the bait shack, where it
dipped and fluttered just like a gull flying against a
strong wind.*

*That was what Ben saw when he woke up. And he
woke up with the sun right on his face, because so much
time had gone by. He didn't mind the sun, though. He
saw the metal gull with its wings flashing. He stuck out
a hand toward it just as though he thought it would
come to him.*

In school Miss Guarino told the class there would be a
Ledgeport Promotion Day to make everyone more aware of
their community and to uphold standards. No one paid this
announcement much attention except Darleen Leeward, who
said it was her father's idea. It would make everyone who lived
in Ledgeport rich off all the people from away who shut up
their summer homes every Labor Day and didn't show up
again until June. Miss Guarino said she doubted Darleen's father meant that exactly, but Darleen insisted she had heard
him talking to all the important people in town to get them
charged up over it.

"He didn't speak to my father," remarked J.J. Bowden, "at
least not that I heard of."

"I said *important* people," Darleen explained. "Probably
someone else will talk to your mom and dad."

Merkka and Lucy exchanged looks. Darleen had a knack for
making kids like J.J. feel crummy.

That afternoon Merkka nagged Gramary to take her to see
the sheep. But Gramary was cutting the side out of the new
bus and couldn't find a stopping place.

"You don't need me," Gramary pointed out. "You know
where Charlie lives."

Merkka tried to get Ben to go with her. But he was sorting scrap metal for Gramary.

Merkka wandered away from the yard. Maybe she would find Lucy and talk her into going to the school playground. But just as she turned up Landing Road, Mom came out of Stan's Market with a bag of groceries and told Merkka they were going to look at a house.

Merkka followed Mom home. "Shouldn't we get Dad to come too?"

Mom shook her head. "We'll just slip out while we can," she said as she set the bag on the kitchen table. "It's the old Haskell Gray house those people fixed up. Now they're moving again, and Ruth Leeward said we can go inside. If it's really good, we'll tell Dad about it afterward."

Merkka and Mom hurried up Church Street to Russell Leeward's office on the green. He was on the phone when they went in, but Margie, his assistant, said he was expecting Beverly and would be right out. They could hear him through the open door to his office. "That's right," he was saying. "Something for everyone. Every single person's got to feel they've got a stake in Ledgeport's future. Promotion? Well, sure, yes, I suppose it's not exactly— Sure, good idea. Sure, a catchy slogan or something. Good, good. We'll be in touch." He slammed down the phone and came striding out to greet Mom and Merkka. "This thing's taking off like wildfire!" he said. "Hear about it today in school, did you?" he asked Merkka. "What do you think, Bev? Make the kids proud to live here. Make them care what this place looks like." His voice dropped. "No need to give up just because the fish plant's closing. Could be a blessing in disguise, the way I see it."

Still talking, he guided them out the door and over to Landing Road. "You'll see," he went on. "We can do better than the plant. A real marina for yachts. Another inn, maybe even a motel. Just have to get a few old-timers to clean up their acts, right?"

They crossed School Street, where Lucy Starobin lived, and turned off Landing Road onto Gray Street.

Mom said, "If you mean Mary, don't expect me to talk her into anything. I have to live with her."

"No, no, Bev. I wouldn't want to put you on the spot with your mother-in-law. There are other ways. Maybe she'll see the light when she realizes the whole town wants to beautify the waterfront. Now," he declared, fishing around a huge key ring, "wait till you see what the Pearlmans did with this house. You'll fall in love with it." He fitted one key, then another, shook the door knob, and finally yanked the door open. They stepped inside.

It was like being in church, where it feels wrong to touch anything or raise your voice. There was something queer about all that empty space. Merkka stayed close to Mom as Mr. Leeward led them through to the kitchen. "Avocado," he informed them. "All your appliances in avocado." Merkka was mystified until she realized he meant the color, which was a kind of dull green. "They're staying with the house because they match the cabinets."

Merkka tried to picture having supper beside a green refrigerator. Only, no, you wouldn't eat in here, because right next door was the dining room, with what Mr. Leeward called a bay window. Merkka looked out at a small lawn and garden. The bay was in the opposite direction downhill from here. But it was a bay window all the same, and it had a shelf in front of it for plants or a cushion. Imagine sitting there. Maybe Lucy would find a shortcut through from School Street, a secret passage between their houses. They could signal to each other with flashlights.

Mr. Leeward showed Mom what had been redone downstairs, and then they went up. The steps were carpeted, and there was a banister that finished in a smooth curl that reminded Merkka of a whelk shell turning in on itself. The bedrooms had wallpaper. Mom kept saying "Uh-huh" to everything Mr. Leeward told her about the house. She touched the switchplate for the light and the faucet on the bathroom sink and the sloping eaves painted to match the paper.

When they came to the yellow room, Merkka knew at once that this was hers. Forget lavender. Here the paper showered the yellow wall with tiny sprays of red and orange flowers. Merkka remained in the room while Mr. Leeward and Mom moved on. Eventually she heard them talking downstairs. Then Mr. Leeward came back up to get her.

"Perfect for you, isn't it?" he said from the doorway.

Merkka nodded.

Merkka and Mom walked home in blissful silence, each going over private thoughts and hopes. But when everyone was in the kitchen at suppertime, Mom acted as though nothing had happened. Dad talked about whether to switch the *Little Mary* over for dragging this fall or to go out scalloping with Norm. Gramary said she hated for the *Little Mary* to have such a strain on her, especially with all the ballast she'd have to carry. She wasn't built for dragging. Mom dished out macaroni and cheese and said anyhow Norm's boat was safer in rough weather and ice.

Then Gramary turned to Merkka and asked how the sheep were today.

"I didn't get there," Merkka blurted. "We went to—"

"We were visiting together," Mom put in with a slight shake of her head.

Merkka fell silent. There must be a good reason why Mom didn't want the Haskell Gray house mentioned. Then Merkka said, "Will Charlie take care of them?"

"He will when he can," Gramary replied. "I'm sure he expects you to help."

"Could you talk to him," Merkka asked her.

"They're not my sheep."

"Come with me tomorrow, Gramary, please. You know what to say."

"We'll see," Gramary told her. "I do need to look over some of his junk. Maybe we'll go after school."

"Me too," said Ben.

"Of course," agreed Gramary. "We need you to help us with the important decisions."

The following afternoon they stood at the old pasture fence on Limeburner Point and tried to count sheep nearly hidden in tall stands of weeds and grasses gone to seed.

Charlie Budge said, "They'll have plenty to eat for a while, but they'll need water out here. When I'm here, I'll do it, but I've work out on the island yet. Mrs. Cope will be coming back as soon as they let her out of the hospital, and there's things to be done for her."

Relieved that Charlie Budge would be absent when she would have to come, Merkka promised fervently to tend the sheep.

"Of course," he said, "you'll have to let Bob Brackett take a few lambs to pay for the hay you'll need later on."

Merkka nodded, but Ben said, "Not my lamb."

"Do you have one picked out?" Gramary asked him.

"Yes," he told her. "His name is Grace."

"Well, not Grace then," Gramary agreed. "You'll have to show us which one when the grass is eaten down some." Starting back toward the barn, she asked Charlie whether he would bring the junk she'd set aside or whether she'd have to use Sam's truck to come fetch the stuff.

"I'll get it to you, Mary," Charlie said, "but I'd just as soon wait till dark."

"Why is that?" she asked, leaning over to drag aside a length of old stove pipe.

"I'd like to stay out of that storm over your way."

Gramary snorted. "Who are you afraid of? Russell Leeward all dressed up like folk from away?"

"Not afraid. Cripes, I'm just not looking for trouble."

Gramary hoisted the stove pipe over her shoulder. "Fine,"

she said. "I'll carry this with me now. You can bring the rest tonight."

"You sure you want to bother with that pipe? It's seen better days."

"Maybe," Gramary told him, "it'll get a new lease on life."

Charlie shrugged, and Gramary and the children set off for home, with Jet weaving from one side of the road to the other on some quest of his own. Gramary called him to her when they stepped out of the way to let a car go by. But once the car had passed, it braked, went into reverse, and backed up until it was abreast of them. Russell Leeward leaned out the window, smiled at Merkka, and asked Gramary if she and Sam were coming by to look at the house.

"What house?" Gramary shifted the stove pipe to the shoulder nearest Mr. Leeward's car.

"Didn't Beverly tell you about the Haskell Gray house?"

Gramary shook her head.

"Well, it's up for sale. Won't be on the market long either."

Gramary said, "I don't know anything about it," and started on down the road.

"Mary!" Mr. Leeward shouted after her. "You should take an interest."

"Why?" she shot back.

"Because things can't go on like they are at the waterfront. We can't put up with it."

"Who's we?"

"A lot of us, Mary. And there's more of us than of all you Weirs and Ingallses and everyone. I tried to talk to Sam. I told him I could get a real good price on your property. Didn't he tell you?"

Ben whispered to Merkka that Jet was going into the bushes across from the ditch. She wanted to hear what Gramary would say. But what if Jet got lost out here? The nearest place he knew was Charlie Budge's.

Merkka clambered into the ditch and up the bank. Then she

called Jet, keeping her voice down, trying to listen to Gramary and Mr. Leeward at the same time. She heard Gramary saying, "Probably knew what I'd say," and then she heard Jet plunging through the undergrowth toward her. She held onto him.

Mr. Leeward shouted, "You're so used to your crud, you don't see it the way everyone else does. You don't notice all that unsightly stuff just left to rot."

"You mean like a dog on the wreck?" Gramary was walking back toward the car now. She still had the stove pipe on her shoulder. "Now that's what I call unsightly. You could turn away from the sight of him, Russ, so you know how it's done." She stopped and slowly shifted the stove pipe again. "If you don't like what you see, don't look." She beckoned Merkka toward her, swung around, and walked on.

"You ought to think about these kids," Mr. Leeward called to her. Merkka, with Ben at her heels, had to pass right by the car. She couldn't help meeting Mr. Leeward's sympathetic gaze. He seemed to be saying that he remembered how much she loved the yellow room. He was on her side. His understanding held her in a kind of trance. She hardly thought about Jet, though she could feel him beside her.

All the rest of the way home she thought about the Haskell Gray house and how it might become their new home. She had a feeling that Russell Leeward was a true friend, even though he and Gramary talked like enemies. Russell Leeward wanted what Merkka wanted, what Mom wanted. So it might really happen, if only they could find a way.

Gramary seemed to forget Russell Leeward as soon as he drove off. She had her mind on her work, and she stayed out in the yard for a while. When she came in late for supper, there were black smudges on her white hair and on her forehead and a distant look in her eyes.

Merkka kept waiting for someone to mention the Haskell Gray house or for Gramary to mention meeting Mr. Leeward, but not a word was spoken about any of those things. Grown-ups could tuck thoughts away like Christmas presents wrapped and hidden. Merkka was bursting to tear into them and find out what was inside. But the talk was about fixing one of the doors on Norm Gray's dragger. Not a door you open and walk through, Merkka knew, but part of the dragging gear. Gramary said she would drop everything to patch it for Norm, and she and Dad discussed whether to weld on a batten or just bead along the crack while it held.

That night Merkka and Mom did the dishes.

"When will you talk about the house?" Merkka whispered as Mom handed her the frying pan.

Mom shook her head. "When the time's right," she whispered back.

"Won't it be too late?"

Mom sighed. "It's complicated." She wiped back a lock of hair, leaving suds like a second eyebrow.

"We saw Mr. Leeward this afternoon. He mentioned the house."

"What did Mary say?"

"Nothing about the house really. About other things."

"Well," Mom answered, "that's something. That's better than nothing." Then she added, "Maybe I'll speak to Dad tonight."

But if she did, Merkka heard none of it, and in the morning Mom didn't want to talk about anything. She put her head in her hands and wouldn't even drink her coffee. Merkka figured she had a headache again.

CHAPTER 12:

Invitations

I felt as though I had invented the Haskell Gray house.
It was exactly, perfectly the one I always pictured. All of
a sudden it seemed possible. Curtains, I thought.
Carpets and a tree with a swing hanging from it. What
could I do to push us a little closer to that house? After
all, I'd pushed Gramary along about the sheep. I had
already helped changes to come our way. The trouble
with Gramary, though, was that when you pushed, you
couldn't be sure what direction she would go in.

Miss Guarino announced that the Ledgeport Board of Selectmen was sponsoring a contest for Ledgeport Appreciation
Day. They had also changed the name of the day from Promotion to Appreciation. The contest was for all ages, and you
could write something or draw or paint or make something.

Lucy wondered whether Darleen Leeward would be allowed
to enter. "In TV contests families who work for the sponsor
can't."

"Darleen doesn't make things anyway," Merkka pointed out. "I saw the invitation she gave Jody yesterday. It's from the Variety Store."

Lucy, who had been sucking the eraser end of her pencil, suddenly bit clear through it. "They say you can stay up all night at Darleen's birthday parties." Then she added, "Everyone's been invited."

"Not everyone," Merkka corrected.

Merkka didn't give Darleen's party another thought until Darleen phoned her that night. Darleen had never ever called her before.

"Don't keep her waiting," said Mom, holding the phone out to Merkka.

Darleen, sounding glum, invited Merkka to the party.

"I don't know," Merkka told her.

At the other end of the line Darleen spoke to someone else, then said into the phone, "Well, are you coming or not?"

Merkka shook her head.

Mom asked, "What is it?"

Without covering the phone, Merkka told Mom, and Mom smiled and nodded.

"Of course you'll go," Mom said. "Remember, it's Darleen's father who can help us."

What did the house have to do with Darleen's birthday? Merkka spoke into the phone. "Did you invite Lucy too?"

"No," said Darleen.

"I can't come," Merkka told her, and hung up.

"What did you do that for?" Mom snapped. She grabbed Merkka's arm so hard her fingers pinched. "Call her back. Tell her you're sorry. Tell her you'll go."

Dad came in from the living room. "What's going on?" His eyes went to Mom's hand still gripping Merkka's arm.

Mom let go and turned away angrily. "She just turned down an invitation to Darleen's birthday party. She was rude."

Dad made a strange face. Merkka couldn't tell whether it was about her being rude or about Darleen's invitation.

"Ruth's my friend," Mom burst out. "And Russ has . . . well, you know what he's trying to do for us."

"Don't let Russ fool you, Bev. He doesn't do for us or anyone. He does *to* us."

Merkka could feel her parents saying more than that without words. What were they talking about? Merkka was sure it had something to do with the Haskell Gray house. After that she hung around downstairs hoping to hear them discuss it, but neither of them mentioned the house or Mr. Leeward at all.

In school the next day Darleen came up to Merkka in the hall and handed her an invitation. It was different from Jody's. Merkka figured that someone had bought it in a hurry first thing this morning.

Merkka waited for Darleen at recess. "I'll come if you ask Lucy."

Darleen shook her head.

"Why not?"

"I don't have to," Darleen told her. "My father made me have you, but he didn't say anything about Lucy, so I won't."

Merkka walked away, leaving the matter up in the air.

That afternoon Mr. Harley Sprague came down the hill to call on Gramary. He waited a long time while Gramary finished the section of fender she was welding. He said, "That's all right" to Ben. He said, "Don't interrupt her" to Merkka.

When Gramary finally set the torch aside and flipped up the eye shield, she didn't seem the least surprised to find him there. "Afternoon," she said. "Something I can do for you?"

"Good afternoon, Mrs. Weir. I came . . . I was hoping we might have a little chat."

"Fine," said Gramary. "What's on your mind?"

Mr. Sprague, looking uncomfortable, waved his hand at the buses and all the tractor and car parts lying around. He talked about the eyesore down here. He said he and his neighbors on the hill would be very much obliged if Gramary would do something about it.

"Eyesore," she repeated thoughtfully. She waved her arm, too, and pointed out into the harbor. "I suppose you'd call the wreck an eyesore. Sticking up out of the water like a corpse."

"Well, no, not exactly. Actually, no, I wouldn't. You see, it's part of the ambiance here."

"The what?"

"The atmosphere. It adds to the scene, if you know what I mean. It's been here for such a long time, it blends in with everything."

Gramary ran her hand through her short white hair. "Where does that put Norm Gray's old dragger?" she asked. "It's been around awhile, but it's not exactly an antique. I always think it looks kind of sickly next to some of those newer fishing boats, especially the steel ones."

Mr. Sprague smiled. "Norman's boat is a fixture around here. Everyone knows it. Everyone knows Norman. That's what you call local color."

Gramary scowled, puzzlement written in every crease around her eyes. "I expect the laundry bothers you. You must see it flapping on the line here when you look down this way."

"Oh, there's nothing wrong with that," Mr. Sprague assured her. "No, that's quite another thing. It's fresh and, well, part of life, you might say."

Gramary nodded, and Mr. Sprague looked encouraged.

"I wonder if I could coax you up for a look from my house. I think you'd understand so much better if you could see what we see from the hilltop. Do come. Bring the children. We'll have some tea."

Merkka had never been inside any of the big houses up the hill. She could remember when they used to be shut up all winter and the big kids said they were haunted. But now people like Mr. Sprague had retired and lived year round in them, and the Billingses had bought one to be the Harbor View Inn.

She held her breath, willing Gramary to accept Mr. Sprague's invitation.

When Gramary nodded and told Jet to stay in the new bus, Merkka and Ben raced ahead of the two grown-ups. Ben didn't know why it was so exciting to be invited up the hill; he was just glad because Merkka was. "Is it a party?" he asked as they stopped in front of the gatepost with a sign in the shape of a clipper ship and the name SPRAGUE on it.

"No," Merkka told him. "There won't be cake or anything."

They waited for Gramary and Mr. Sprague before going past the gate. Everyone's feet crunched on the even pebbles that surfaced the curving driveway.

"It sounds like snow," Ben declared.

Mr. Sprague laughed. Merkka felt tight between her shoulders.

"What did I say?" Ben whispered to her.

"Nothing. It doesn't matter," she whispered back.

As soon as they entered the house, Merkka realized that it wasn't nearly as grand as some she saw on TV. Yet it gleamed with a soft luster. Floors and furniture were spotless. The rugs were muted browns and greens, the upholstered furniture white. She glanced into one room with books on every wall, but it was the big white room that Mr. Sprague led them into. There they stood before a large glass door and gazed out over the harbor.

The whole world was out there, or at least all of Merkka's world. She could see all the way to the fish plant. She could see the Variety Store and Stan's Market and the church steeple and the roof of the Town Hall. She could see the monument and the wreck and the Porcupines off Tinkers Island. She could even see part of Grace Island, and beyond, with parts of Sheep and Moose Islands showing too. And she could see Gramary's yard, with Dad's bait shack out toward the old landing, and she could especially see the two buses side by side and the weapons carrier and the Hudson and what was left of

Brackett's manure spreader that was beyond fixing but not beyond salvage.

Someone brought tea on a tray while Merkka was staring out at the scene below Mr. Sprague's house. She heard him ask for cake. Cake! She glanced around quickly, intending to hush Ben before he made a big deal about it. But Ben was lost in another wonder, going from one painting to another. He stood transfixed before a storm scene. Merkka noticed that the details blurred when she came up close to it. Merkka grabbed Ben's hand because she was afraid he would try to touch that painting.

Mr. Sprague opened the big glass door and handed each of the children a napkin with a slice of cake on it. Ben wanted to go back and examine a painting of a cracked jug with some kind of vine overspreading it, but Merkka steered him out to the terrace to a white table.

"Sit down," she ordered.

"Why?"

"You might make a mess. He might be watching."

"There isn't anything to mess with," he pointed out. "No frosting." He left the cake and walked over to a wooden tub with orange flowers in it.

"Don't you want your cake?" Merkka called after him.

He shook his head. His hand closed over a flower head. Then he walked down the steps to the lawn with his hand cupped as if the flower were still there.

Merkka quickly devoured Ben's cake. She crushed both napkins, then didn't know what to do with them.

"Merkka!" Ben called.

She found him looking at a metal thing that might have been a windmill, only it wasn't. It had wings or paddles that looked like flat lollipops. "Don't touch it," she said.

"I wasn't. Why not?"

"It's some kind of machine. It might start up."

"What kind?" he asked, more drawn to it now that it had a possible function.

She probably knew less about machines than Ben did, since he spent so much time with Gramary under engine hatch covers or dismantling old cars. "A generator," she declared, the word just coming to her out of nowhere.

Ben was impressed. He stared at it. Then a look of doubt crept into his eyes. "Are you sure?"

"Of course not," she said.

When Gramary and Mr. Sprague joined them, they were still regarding the "generator" with uneasy fascination.

Gramary took in the "generator" as she spoke. "Let me see if I've got this straight. You don't object to boats of any kind, even landbound, even wrecks. Is that right?"

"Right. They're what one expects to see in a small Maine fishing village."

"You don't even object to Spike's dried codfish hanging off the shed roof."

"Right."

Gramary's eye never left the "generator." "Or boat cradles in the summer and mooring blocks hauled ashore in the winter."

"Right, right."

Far below, on the line stretched between the Hudson car and the old school bus, Dad's shirts and pants filled like balloons in a sudden waft of air and then sagged limply.

"Also," added Gramary musingly, "the laundry."

"Of course. You see, it's in its proper place."

Gramary turned her full attention to the "generator." "What have we here?" she asked.

"It's a sculpture by Piers Johannsen," Mr. Sprague informed her. "He calls it *Tree of Life*."

"Ah," said Gramary.

Ben asked what a tree of life was for.

Mr. Sprague laughed the way he had earlier. "It's art," he said. "For art's sake. To make sense of the senseless, to give meaning."

Ben shot a look at Merkka, who avoided his glance and stared at *Tree of Life*. Gramary wiped her hands on her overalls, a sign that she was ready to move on.

"Thank you so much for coming," Mr. Sprague said to her. "For giving me a chance to plead my case."

"That's all right," Gramary replied.

"And you'll try . . . try to clean things up down there?"

"It'll be bit by bit," Gramary told him. "You might not notice much change for a while. It'll take some planning, work."

"I appreciate that, Mrs. Weir. I really do. I told Russell you could be—" He broke off, then quickly explained. "Of course we've talked about this. He's deeply concerned about the image we present, all of us."

Gramary gazed at *Tree of Life*. She said she expected things would be some different by next summer.

Mr. Sprague nodded and smiled and ushered them down the crunchy driveway.

"Thank you for the cake," Merkka said. She yanked Ben's cuff. "Thank him," she whispered.

"I didn't have any cake," Ben retorted at full voice. "You can thank him twice."

Her ears burning, Merkka trudged on ahead. She thought Gramary would thank Mr. Sprague, too, and set an example for Ben the way Mom would, but Gramary had no more to say just now. She was deep in thought all the way down the steep hill and barely looked up when Cliff Billings passed them in his car and waved a friendly greeting.

CHAPTER 13:

On the Line

*When Mrs. Cope started to pay Ben for picking plastic
junk off Grace Island, I decided to keep all the foam
stuff that's used on boats for flotation. I brought every
piece home and hid it under my bed. Every once in a
while I borrowed tape from Dad's tool box, the tape he
uses to hold together broken exhaust pipes. I began to
stick the Styrofoam on the underneath of my bed. It
never held too well because the springs that hold the
mattress are mostly spaces. They move when you sit
and roll over. Then the tape comes loose and the
Styrofoam falls off. One day when it was all hanging
down, Mom came sweeping and saw what was
underneath my bed. She threw it away.*

*"Some crazy, wasteful game," she reported to Dad.
"You'd think duct tape grew on trees."*

"Where does it come from?" Ben wanted to know.

Dad talked about aluminum and I stopped listening.
But later on, when Gramary and I were alone, she
brought it up. "Flotation?"
I nodded. I could see she was thinking, not scolding.
"You need a lot of it to keep an iron bed afloat," I
explained.
She said she expected you did.
Then I was embarrassed, because I could tell Gramary
had guessed why I was doing it. I tried to pretend that
all that tape and flotation was from a long time ago. I
tried to act as though I'd nearly forgotten about it.

After their visit up the hill, there was no holding Ben back.
Everything he had seen and heard at Mr. Sprague's came tumbling out at suppertime. That started Mom talking about the
Haskell Gray house and Dad talking about Russell Leeward's
interest in the property. Then Gramary dropped a remark
about Russ having set Harley Sprague on her.

Dad said, "I think you can expect a good deal of pressure
from now on."

"They can't force me to sell," Gramary replied.

"They can shut you down," Dad warned.

Mom leaned toward Gramary. "We could do something else
with this place. Listen, Mary, I've been thinking a lot about it.
A family business right here, lobster rolls and fried clams. Not
a fancy restaurant, nothing big."

Gramary regarded her thoughtfully. "It's not out of the question, Bev. But I'm not ready, not yet. Not while that twerp Russell Leeward is leaning on me. I'll give him a run for his money
first."

"But you'll consider it?" Mom pressed. "It would mean moving. To convert this place, you know. But Russ says even if we
sell only part of the waterfront property, we'd make enough to

buy a nice house and set up the snack bar." She stopped when Dad placed his hand on hers.

"Ma needs time," he cautioned. "She's right too. It's not altogether over with the fish plant either. Norm says there's talk about someone starting a new plant, processing sea clams, looking for the right place."

Gramary shook her head. "They'll need a deepwater port for those dredgers. Anyway, we're too far off the beaten track."

"And there are other problems," Mom added. "Just like with fishmeal. You won't have tourists if you've got that smell. It won't be like it used to. We've got to think about getting people behind us, not against us."

Merkka thought that made a lot of sense. It occurred to her that if she went to Darleen's birthday, she might have a chance to hint that Gramary's attitude was changing. That could encourage Mr. Leeward to hold onto the Haskell Gray house for them.

So the next day, which was the day before Darleen's birthday, Merkka told Darleen she would come to her party. Darleen nodded. It was clear she didn't care one way or the other. Merkka told Lucy she had held out as long as she could, hoping to get invitations for both of them. She promised to save something from the party for Lucy. But Lucy said she didn't want anything from snobby Darleen.

"I won't have fun," Merkka promised.

But Lucy clammed up and wouldn't speak to her for the rest of the day.

That put Merkka in such a bad mood that when she came home and found Ben using her pad of paper to draw pictures, she stormed at him. He had no right to take it without asking. He was wasting paper anyway. Jet, on his way to greet her, stopped short, then turned and crawled into the narrow space between the table and the wall.

Ben just stared at her dumbfounded until she burst into tears. Then he went to sit beside Jet with his thumb in his mouth and Jet's ear against his cheek.

Merkka wanted to tell him she was sorry. She said, "I need my paper to practice for the contest. It's very important. I might win a prize."

Ben listened guardedly.

"You can make a picture for the contest too," she offered. "But you have to erase your mistakes, not start over each time."

Ben nodded. He came out from behind the table and said, "Come and see what Gramary made."

Relieved that he was talking to her again, Merkka followed him down the outside stairs to the yard. Jet came, too, but he kept his distance from Merkka.

"Look," said Ben, pointing at the clothes on the line.

She looked around and past them. There wasn't anything special to see. "Where?" she said. "What?"

"Shirt," he told her.

Her eyes returned to the clothesline. And then she noticed it, the gray and black swirls setting it apart from the other shirts, its permanently full sleeves bulging from a nonexistent wind. "What is it?" she asked, but already she knew. It was sculpture. Not a *Tree of Life*, but a shirt with wrinkled stove-pipe arms and a front made of fender that billowed just like a real shirt body. It even had a collar with one tip up, buttons made of washers, and a patch on one of the elbows.

Gramary came out of the buses. "Don't say anything about it," she said to the children. "I want to see who notices."

"Ben showed me," Merkka said. And then, with admiration, "How did you do that, Gramary?"

"It was fun," Gramary answered. "A break from the hard work. Like Ben's frog. Ben, where did you put the frog I made you?"

Ben dashed off and returned with a frog on a lily pad, all of it made from scrap metal. Merkka recognized one or two pieces she had picked up on Grace Island. The best part was the frog's warty back and its eyes made of bulging rivets.

"See," Ben pointed out, "this part's my broken car."

And so it was. It had broken so long ago that Merkka had forgotten about it. Gramary had said she would get around to fixing it one day. Now here it was, returned to its owner, transformed into a frog.

Gramary never made things like that for Merkka. "Ben's lucky," she said.

"Ben doesn't own a whole flock of sheep," Gramary reminded her. "A flock of sheep that needs watering, by the way. Charlie's gone out to the island to be Mrs. Cope's caretaker for a few days. You'll have to take care of the sheep."

Ben kept Merkka and Jet company going out to Limeburner Point. He brought his frog along. But Gramary's marvelous shirt stayed put on the line among the cloth ones that Mr. Harley Sprague had no objection to.

It hung there waiting to be noticed.

CHAPTER 14:

One Good Tern

*I couldn't help thinking that the only thing that kept us
from moving into the Haskell Gray house was Gramary.
I wanted to go back and look at it again all by myself,
but I was afraid I might discover something wrong with
it. I tried to remember whether I had seen stone under
the steps. All I could be sure of was the wooden slats
woven like a basket. But that wouldn't be enough to
hold up a house. There had to be a real foundation
behind those slats, something that was solid and deep as
a ledge.*

Saturday morning was overcast and chilly. Mom lay on the sofa
looking at a magazine. Dad was out lobster fishing. Ben and
Gramary were down in the buses.

Merkka tried to get Mom to talk about the Haskell Gray
house, but she just covered her eyes with the back of her
hand. All she wanted was peace and quiet.

Merkka said, "I have to bring Darleen a present."

Mom groaned. Then she told Merkka to fetch her purse from the kitchen. She had to sit up to dig out some money, which she thrust at Merkka. "Find something at the Variety Store," she said.

"I don't know what to get. Come with me."

"No. Lucy can help you decide."

Merkka shook her head. "Lucy wasn't invited." She waited for Mom to exclaim over Lucy being left out. Mom just yawned and lay back again. "And get me a little bag of peanuts," she said. "Salted."

Merkka went to find Ben. He was watching Gramary cut a whole section of roof out of the new bus to match a section already missing from the old one. Merkka said, "Won't it rain in?"

Gramary grunted as she yanked out the framing she had cut through. "It'll be closed up again when I'm done."

Merkka wondered why Gramary would go to the trouble of making holes in her roof if she didn't want them, but she knew better than to ask. "Come with me," she said to Ben. "I have to get something at the Variety Store."

When Ben stood up, something dropped from his lap. It looked like a metal bird. It looked like a tern, its swallow tail and wings poised in flight. Merkka picked it up. She could tell it was made from leftover fender.

"You want that?" Gramary asked her.

"Oh, yes. Could I give it to Darleen?"

"Darleen Leeward?" Gramary's pliers came crashing down. Ben ran to pick them up for her and climbed a bus seat to hand them over.

"It's her birthday, and I need a present."

"You think she'd like it?"

"I don't know what she likes, but I think it's wonderful. So could I?"

Gramary told Merkka she could do what she liked with it.

Merkka carried it to the yard. "How did she do it?" she asked Ben.

"She just cut," he said, "and then she used the torch and then the tinsnips. Then she hammered it over a pipe. Like that." He pointed to the metal shirt. The real clothing was gone from the line. Somehow, all alone like that, the shirt looked even more real, but almost scary that way. Like a picture. No, like sculpture. Merkka looked down at the tern. Close up, there were no fine details of a bird; yet it seemed to be every swooping and diving tern she had ever seen.

She carried it into the house and up to her bedroom.

"Did you get my peanuts?" Mom called after her.

Merkka tore down the stairs and returned the money. "I didn't have to go. Gramary made something. It's gorgeous."

Mom rose slowly and made her way to the kitchen, where she rummaged around until she found an open bag of corn chips.

As the day wore on, Merkka began to worry about the present. She ran upstairs a dozen times to look at it. She swung between loving it and wishing it was hers for keeps and imagining Darleen running her fingers over the rough edge of the wings and then depositing it out of sight. Merkka took the tern down to the bathroom and washed it. Then she asked Mom for some polish.

Mom said there might be something under the kitchen sink. Merkka found some white stuff in a jar. She scrubbed the tern with it and rinsed it, but the metal was no shinier. Then she had a brilliant idea. She asked Mom if she could use a little of her nail polish.

"What for?" Mom sounded as though she were about to say no.

"It's for Darleen's. I won't make a mess."

Mom said she could take some from her bureau. "Just a little."

The nail polish was dark red and shiny. Merkka started out

with the idea of just painting the beak red. Then there would be no mistake about it being the beak of a tern. But she dropped some of the nail polish on one wing. When she tried to wipe it, it smeared, so she quickly brushed more red to cover the wing. After that she had to make the other wing match. But that left the body looking naked and dull, so she lacquered that as well. The tern really had a sheen now, like those little lobster buoys next to postcards and notepaper at the Variety Store.

After painting the tern, the only thing Merkka had to worry about was what to wear and what to bring for overnight. Lucy had a special bag that matched her sleeping bag. Merkka didn't even have a sleeping bag.

"Borrow Lucy's," Mom suggested.

"I can't," said Merkka. "Lucy wasn't invited."

"Which means she won't be needing it herself."

Merkka couldn't explain what was wrong with Lucy not going. Eventually she stuffed her hairbrush and toothbrush and pajamas into her pillow case, rolled the tern in a towel, and shoved it on top of everything else.

Just before it was time to go, Merkka got cold feet about the tern, even with the nail polish on it, and decided to buy Darleen a puzzle or a scarf with Maine scenes on it.

"I need some money," she told Mom, who had her head in the refrigerator and was mumbling about supper. "For the present. I just decided."

Mom said one present was enough.

Merkka ran out to Gramary, who had put together some of the pieces she had cut out of the ceilings of the buses. Merkka looked down the arched pipes and saw they had become legs of something. She said, "Would it be all right to keep the tern for myself? I really like it a lot. I might like it better than Darleen would."

"Fine with me," Gramary told her.

"Only then I need to get Darleen something else."

Gramary fished in her side pocket and pulled out a couple of dollar bills. "That enough?"

Merkka raced up to Water Street, but the Variety Store had already closed. She ran to Stan's Market. They didn't have anything like a present, so she bought bubble gum. She trudged back down to the house, where Mom was frying fish and Gramary and Ben were washing up.

"All set?" Gramary asked.

"Yes. No. I don't know. I guess I shouldn't keep the tern when it would be such a special present."

Mom caught on to what they were saying. She scolded Merkka for taking money from Gramary when she already had something for Darleen, and she scolded Gramary for spoiling the children. Then she noticed that Merkka was late for the party. She made Merkka put on her best dress and she emptied out the pillow case and put just the pajamas and toothbrush and hairbrush in a plastic bag with handles.

Merkka retrieved the tern and shoved it into the bag as well. If only she hadn't said she would go to that dumb party. She said, "It's too cold for this dress."

Mom told her to get going.

"Goodbye," she said to Ben.

"Merkka!" Mom exclaimed.

Merkka saw Jet get up, ready to follow her. "Oh, goodbye," she told him. She knelt down and flung her arms around his neck.

"That dog's rolled in something. You'll get your dress dirty," Mom objected, pulling her up and sending her out the door.

Merkka had to go all the way to the other side of the green to get to Quarry Road. That meant crossing School Street where the Starobins lived. What if she just turned right onto it and went in and stayed overnight with Lucy? She slowed, thinking about it. Only she knew that if she didn't show up at Darleen's, Mrs. Leeward would call Mom.

Sighing, Merkka walked on by. As soon as she passed the

church, she began to hear the kids at Darleen's, out in the backyard where the patio was. Then she saw some of them at the end of the Leewards' driveway. The first thing she noticed was that they were all wearing jeans and sweaters.

She stopped where she was. Quickly she pulled the tern out of the plastic bag and stuck it under a lilac bush. Back on the driveway, she watched everyone for a moment until Jody caught sight of her and ran to meet her. It was getting dark and it was already cold, but the hot dogs and hamburgers smelled delicious out there. She couldn't help being drawn in. Darleen's mother even found a warm sweater for her to wear, because Darleen wanted to fool around in the dark for a while before they went in for birthday cake.

They took turns thinking up names of people everyone knew and sticking one on the back of a girl and answering questions until she guessed who it was. Most names were boys in school. Some were teachers and singers and TV stars. It was fun laughing at wrong guesses, and for a while Merkka laughed just as hard as all the others.

When it was her turn to have a name taped on her back, there was a lot of whispering and giggling first. Then they told her to think of someone close. When she guessed Lucy, she didn't even raise a laugh. Next she tried Miss Guarino, but they had already done her for another kid. She was stumped then. Desperate, she named Jay, Lucy's brother who was in high school. That made everyone shriek and dance around her. She was getting tired of the game, tired of being laughed at. Darleen showed up with a broom, which she rode around the barbecue. A horse? But Merkka didn't know any horses.

Finally they told her to think of what flew on broomsticks.

"I get it!" she cried. "Witches."

"Think of just one."

"One witch," she repeated helplessly.

"Someone old."

The oldest person she could think of, even older than Reggie Ingalls, was Mrs. Cope, but she wasn't a witch.

"Come on, Merkka. Old. Close to home."

"I give up," she told them. She could feel the sweater pull out where someone peeled the tape from her back. Then the paper was thrust before her eyes. She had to take it under the patio light to read the name: *Mary Weird—Waterfront Witch.* But what did it mean? "Me?" she asked.

"No, stupid," Darleen shouted, "your grandma. She's the witch."

"Who says?"

"My father!" Darleen screeched, and she doubled over, laughing.

Merkka stood very still while the laughter caught like flames all around her.

"Don't feel bad," Jody said to her. "It was just a joke."

Merkka nodded. "I know." Everyone was trooping inside now. There would be cake with candles and loud music and more screaming. Suddenly Merkka shook off the sweater. She pulled it down her arms, leaving the sleeves inside out. "Could you give this to Mrs. Leeward?" she said to Jody. "I have to go home now."

Jody said, "Don't you want any cake?"

Merkka did, very much. She wanted to see whether it was store-bought from the mall and had roses and writing on it. "I have to go," she told Jody. "I didn't know we'd be so late."

"But the party's for overnight."

"I'm late," Merkka declared as she turned and made her way out to Quarry Road. If she went back for her plastic bag, that would give away the fact that she had meant to stay. Her breath came short, as if she had been running. She heard them singing "Happy Birthday" inside, and stopped a moment to listen. Her knees wanted to cave in. They seemed to be the first part of Merkka to take in the awful realization that Mary Weird would be stuck to her, never mind the tape, for the rest of her life.

How could Gramary stand being so unpopular that people called her a witch? Didn't she know? Didn't she care?

Suddenly Merkka remembered the tern. Feeling her way toward the lilac bush, she groveled around its roots.

"Merkka?"

It was Mr. Leeward with a flashlight. She stood up to face him.

"Jody told me," he said. "I'm real sorry. It wasn't meant the way it sounds. Darleen overheard something. She didn't understand. So why don't you come on in now and have some cake?"

"I have to go home," Merkka told him. She was beginning to shiver.

He reached out to her. "Do you like secrets? Darleen does. Let's you and me have one, okay? Let's not say anything that'll make anyone mad or, you know, upset."

Merkka said, "I have to go home."

"Your mother thinks you're staying. What'll you tell her?"

Merkka's teeth began to chatter.

Mr. Leeward sighed. "I'd better drive you then. You can't be out alone this late. Come on." He put his arm around her and steered her toward his car.

She was grateful to him. He didn't say much more, only that maybe she could help convince her dad to convince her grandmother about selling the waterfront property.

"Dad couldn't do without his bait shack," she said.

"It wouldn't have to be the whole place," Mr. Leeward assured her. As he slowed in front of her house, she edged away from him. "Think of it," he insisted. "If you and me play our cards right, this time next year I might be driving you home to Gray Street." He leaned across her to open the door. "We'll keep that between you and I for now, though, won't we."

She said, "Yes, Mr. Leeward. Thank you for bringing me home."

"That's all right. Mrs. Leeward was real worried when you didn't come in with the other girls."

Merkka knew she was supposed to say something about being sorry to have worried Mrs. Leeward, but she just ran to her house. The kitchen floor seemed to roll under her feet as if it were afloat. She drew a deep breath and took in the smell of Dad's boots and the sourness around the kitchen sink. Jet came weaving over to her, and she hugged him until the boat feeling went away.

There was a light on in the living room, but only Gramary was there.

"I thought you were staying overnight," Gramary said.

"I changed my mind."

"Early start tomorrow," Gramary told her with a yawn.

"Where are we going?"

"I am. Out to the island. Mrs. Cope's coming back for a while before she goes to Florida. She'll need some help out there. You'll have to see to the sheep for a bit."

"Who will take care of Ben?" Merkka asked.

"Your mom will work something out. It won't be too long. You'd better go up now. It's late."

Merkka said, "I know. That's why Mr. Leeward drove me home." She stopped on the stairs. "Gramary, why don't you like him?"

Gramary moaned. "Can't hardly explain. Seems like he's always after something. Even when he was a kid, he was that way."

"Like Charlie Budge?"

"No," Gramary declared. "Nothing like Charlie and his foolish schemes."

Merkka continued on up the stairs. There were so many people Gramary found fault with, there didn't seem much point trying to sort one from another. Stabbing the darkness to find her bed, she pricked her finger on something sharp. She waved around until she caught the string for the overhead light. When she turned it on, Ben twisted under his covers and made a sucking noise, but he didn't wake up. There on Merkka's pillow was another metal bird. It looked like a tern, too, only this one had its head arched over its breast as though preening. Its fine beak pierced a scrap of paper with numbers and structural diagrams penciled on one side and a note from Gramary on the other. The note was about watering the sheep at Charlie's place. After that, Gramary had written: "One good tern deserves another."

Merkka set the preening tern on the floor next to her bed. She went to the head of the stairs. "Gramary?" she whispered. No one stirred, upstairs or down. "Jet," she called softly. Magic words, she thought. "Good boy, come!" she said in a stronger voice. She heard his claws on the floor and thumps as he started up the stairs.

"Good boy," she whispered. Turning out the light and climbing into bed, she patted the space beside her. He landed lightly and settled, long and warming, inside the curve of her body. She wasn't going to take any chances with him going out with Gramary and Dad in the early morning and maybe being left on the island with Charlie Budge. "Good boy," she murmured, breathing in the furry softness of his ruff. It smelled of rockweed and starfish.

CHAPTER 15:

Sticks and Stones

*When Ben began to draw pictures, everyone said he was
an artist. They said he took after Gramary, who could
make things out of trash that looked good enough for
Mrs. Cope to put over her fireplace. Once I asked
Gramary what I was good at. "Words," she said. "You're
a good talker."*

By the time Merkka woke up, a driving rain spattered the windows and drummed overhead. Ben was on the floor playing with Jet, who had already been out and was just beginning to dry off.

"Was the party fun?" Ben asked her.

"It was all right."

Merkka heard voices downstairs. Then Mom called up to her to come down. Merkka pulled on her jeans and a shirt and padded downstairs in her socks, left on overnight. Mrs. Leeward stood just inside the kitchen door. She was wearing a raincoat and was dressed for church.

"I just came by to drop off your bag," she told Merkka.

Merkka said thank you.

Mom said, "Ruth tells me you left without saying goodbye."

"I said goodbye to Mr. Leeward. He drove me home."

Mrs. Leeward spoke quickly. "Russ says she wanted to get home like anything. He says they had a real nice talk on the way. Isn't that right, Merkka?"

Merkka thought about the talk. About secrets. "I guess so."

Mrs. Leeward added, "I brought you a piece of birthday cake. I hope it didn't get wet."

Merkka said, "Thank you very much."

"Well, I've got to go. We're ushering this morning. Have to be prompt."

Mom said, "Tell Russ thanks for bringing Merkka home. Maybe one of these Sundays you'll see me in church again."

"You're looking a whole lot better," Mrs. Leeward remarked. "Haven't seen you looking this good in the morning for a while."

Mom nodded. "Getting back to normal."

After the door closed, Merkka asked, "Were you sick?"

"No," said Mom, "not really. Why didn't you stay overnight at Darleen's?"

"I didn't want to," Merkka told her. "Is Dad hauling traps today, or did he just take Gramary out to the island?"

"He's planning on getting the traps in the Narrows, but it may blow up too hard. I told him I'd like for him to come straight back."

Merkka gazed out the window. The wind was coming from behind the hill. All the boats in the harbor faced it on taut lines. A dismal day ahead. "Could we do something?" Merkka asked Mom. "Could we bake cookies or a cake the way we used to do?"

"No need to bake when you've just been given a hunk of birthday cake."

"Not for eating," Merkka explained. "For fun."

Mom shook her head. "I don't want anything to do with

food." Then her voice softened. "Maybe later. I won't mind by this afternoon. You can ask Lucy over if you want."

Merkka started for the phone, then recalled that Lucy was mad at her. She said, "I'll do the sheep first."

"What, in this rain? They shouldn't need water today."

"I'm supposed to check, though. To be sure they're all right."

"It beats me," Mom declared, "how you and your grandmother can get mixed up in a bunch of wild sheep that no one else wants."

"Charlie Budge wanted them," Merkka pointed out.

"Charlie is an old fool," Mom exclaimed.

"I can sell some. It might help to buy the Haskell Gray house."

Mom shot a look at her. "Don't hold your breath about that house. Between your father and your grandmother dragging their heels, it'll probably change hands two or three times over before we can do anything about it."

"But Mr. Leeward says there's a good chance we'll get it."

"When? When did he say that?"

"Last night when he drove me home."

Mom frowned. "He doesn't know Mary like I do."

Merkka struggled with what she didn't dare say. She came out with, "Someone called her a witch."

"Who did?"

"Kids. They heard it. What do they mean?"

"Don't pay any attention. Forget about it."

"All right," Merkka said, pulling on her foul-weather jacket. "Only I don't know how to."

"Just remember," Mom told her, setting boots out in front of the door, "sticks and stones can break your bones but names can never hurt you." She made Merkka fold her pants legs inside the boots.

Merkka called Jet. There was a tumbling sound and a wail from Ben. Jet came bounding and slipping down the stairs.

"Why did you do that?" Ben shouted to her. "You spoiled my fort."

"I'm sorry," she called.

"Jet was my dragon. He was inside the fort."

"I'm sorry," Merkka yelled up to Ben. "You can have a piece of Darleen's birthday cake. Okay?"

The phone rang. It was Lucy, who wanted to hear about the party.

"It was all right," Merkka told her.

"What kind of cake?"

"I don't know," Merkka answered, averting her eyes from the wrapped piece that Mrs. Leeward had brought. "I didn't stay."

"Oh," said Lucy. Merkka could hear her whispering to someone. "Can I come over?"

"I'm going out to the sheep. I'll come get you afterward."

"Okay," said Lucy.

"Okay," said Merkka, her spirits lifting in spite of the dreary day. She and Jet splashed out into it.

She decided that soaked sheep don't look as healthy as dry sheep. How could she tell if one of them was ailing? Besides, the rain spooked them. They wouldn't let her close. Jet kept swinging around behind them until she gave up and said, "Good boy. That'll do."

They trudged back into town and over to Lucy's. Mrs. Starobin made them wait on the porch while she brought towels, and then she told Merkka to strip down before she came in.

"Out here?" she protested.

"No one's looking," Mrs. Starobin assured her as she held out a big towel to wrap around her. There was a towel for Jet, too, but Mrs. Starobin made him stay out on the porch.

Merkka, with Lucy's bathrobe on, went into the kitchen, which smelled of coffee and something pungent and hot. There were newspapers lying around and an open book on the table. In Lucy's house there was always something to read. Sometimes Mr. Starobin would say, "Listen to this!" And then everyone would stop what they were doing while he read aloud from his book.

Today Lucy and Merkka sat on the floor and played Go Fish. Lucy was full of questions about the party. But it was Mrs. Starobin who asked, "What name was taped to your back?"

Merkka drew a long breath. "It was silly," she said. "It didn't mean anything." She looked at the cards in her hand and said to Lucy, "Do you have any eights?"

"You just asked for eights," Lucy said.

Mrs. Starobin handed Merkka her jeans, all warm from the dryer.

Mr. Starobin looked up from his book. "What didn't mean anything?"

So Merkka couldn't avoid telling them without making a big deal over it.

Mrs. Starobin said, "They probably overheard someone."

"My mother says to forget it," Merkka told them. "She says names can never hurt."

Mr. Starobin stood up. "When names are weapons, they can hurt."

No one spoke for a moment. Then Lucy asked what Merkka had said to the kids.

Merkka shrugged. She couldn't remember exactly. "I didn't really know what they meant."

Mr. Starobin said, "It meant that your grandmother's bugging someone, that's all. Everyone in Ledgeport thinks the world of her." He started talking about people in town and Ledgeport Appreciation Day. He said Russell Leeward was pretty heavy-handed about it. Merkka remembered that Gramary had made a wonderful owl out of scrap metal for the Starobins' boat. It was to keep gulls from dirtying it, but Lucy had said that her dad thought it was a work of art.

Lucy took Merkka into the dining room to look at her model of the town green that she was making out of cardboard for the contest. She hadn't begun to paint any of it yet, but already it looked terrific.

"What are you doing for a project?" Mr. Starobin asked Merkka.

"Nothing," she told him. "I'm no good at things like this."

"You could find a poem that you like and write it down and make a border for it that's appropriate." He went away and then returned with a couple of books.

She looked at them doubtfully. "Which ones are about Ledgeport?" she wanted to know.

"None," Mr. Starobin told her. "And some."

Merkka opened one of the books. Many of the poems were so short that she began to wonder whether she might be able to write a poem herself. "They don't rhyme," she said. "This one has hardly any words in it." Then she looked through the other book. "Here's a long one," she said. "I don't even know where it ends." Then she saw that it was about war. "It doesn't have anything to do with Ledgeport," she said. She went on, looking at a line here and a line there. And then, all of a sudden, she found herself reading a poem from start to finish. It was called "Maine." It was about Gramary's yard and the Bracketts and even Charlie Budge and Ed Ingalls. It was about everything Ben loved and thought beautiful. She was amazed. The poet must have stood in the middle of Gramary's old cars to write about them like that.

"Mr. Starobin," she yelled, "listen to this! It's about us. It's about truck panels and tractors, and there's even a Hudson car in it."

"Okay," he called from the second floor landing, "shoot!"

She looked up to see him with his face covered with white foam. She began to read, "'When old cars get retired, they go to Maine. . . .'"

"Think you can draw a picture of that?" he asked when she came to the end of the poem.

Her excitement started to leak away at the thought of trying to draw anything. "My little brother could," she told him.

Mr. Starobin disappeared a moment, then reappeared with

his face clear. "Sounds like a team project then. You be the master designer and Ben can be the draftsman."

"What's a draftsman?" both girls asked at once.

"The guy who does the actual drawing."

"But what would I really be doing?" Merkka asked warily.

"Making such a good hand-printed copy that someone will want to frame it and hang it in his house. You'll have to practice. I'll show you about margins and spacing. You'll need good paper."

"That sounds great," Lucy encouraged. "Then we'll both have projects."

Merkka wasn't at all sure, but she did copy down the poem so she could read it to Ben. In the middle of it, it came to her that there wasn't anything beautiful in it. She asked Mr. Starobin whether she could find a prettier poem.

He looked over at her copying. He was reading the poem to himself. "Nothing wrong with that," he told her. "You know what beauty is?"

She shook her head.

"Truth," he said. "And that is all you need to know."

"Are you sure?" she demanded.

"Pretty sure. I'm not the first person to have said it."

Merkka finished copying the poem, but secretly she wondered about writing one of her own, not about engine blocks and old cars, thick as cows, grazing behind frame barns. Maybe, if she tried hard enough, she would be able to write something about the light over the water and the islands riding high on it and the porpoises slicing through it on a calm day. Maybe she would write a small poem about the winter moon freezing the bay in its cold, hard beam.

She and Lucy and Jet went home through the rain. At midday Dad called in on the radiophone. It was blowing hard. He was anchored in the back cove off Grace Island and was thinking of laying over there. Relieved, Mom was in a rare good mood. She let Lucy and Merkka make brownies, and they all had supper around the TV, watching a movie. Then Mom put Ben to bed on Gramary's sofa so that Lucy and Merkka could have the upstairs room to themselves.

"This is what it will be like when we move," Merkka confided to Lucy. "You can come over whenever you want, because I'll have my own room, and it's yellow." And Mom will be happy like this, Merkka thought to herself, the way she used to be before she started to worry all the time and feel crummy.

In the morning it was blowing just as hard as ever. Jet came back inside almost as soon as Mom put him out. Her good mood was over now. She was anxious to get going so that she could drop Ben off at Ruth Leeward's for the day. She left Merkka and Lucy to their own breakfasts and told them to make lunches as well.

They made peanut butter sandwiches on brownies, even though the brownies tended to come apart when they spread the peanut butter.

"Extras," suggested Lucy. "We can trade them."

Lucy was right. They did a brisk business at lunchtime, and ended up with potato chips and a pen with a light at the end of it and two packages of M&Ms.

After school Lucy went to her house to work on her town green, and Merkka ran home to let Jet out. He was overjoyed to see her after being alone all day. The house seemed awfully big, so Merkka and Jet fooled around and made a lot of noise in it. Then she got some paper and a pencil and sat down at the kitchen table to write a poem. Nothing came to her. Think of summer, she told herself. "When skies are blue," she began, "the boats come through." Now what? "When skies are gray," she went on, "they stay away." Jet sidled up to her and nudged her elbow.

She went into the living room and looked out the window. The first thing she tried to see was the *Little Mary* on her mooring. All her life she had learned to check the boat before looking for or at anything else. There was such a chop out in the harbor she couldn't even find the mooring buoy. The other boats were bobbing and swinging on their lines.

Next she walked to the window overlooking the yard. Jet pushed past her to stand at the door. She saw a yellow slicker just disappear inside the buses. Maybe Dad was home after all and *Little Mary* was secured at the float. Maybe Jet could hear him.

Merkka threw on her foul-weather jacket again and made her way carefully down the steep outside stairs. Jet, at her heels, ducked right and left to get past her, then waited for her at the bottom. He seemed afraid of the metal shirt, maybe because it whipped and jounced so wildly on the line.

"Dad?" she called. She came around the front of the buses and heard two voices inside them. For some reason, she held back. It could easily be Spike and Ed looking for something. They would help themselves to Gramary's things just the way she did to theirs.

Merkka moved back until she was below one of the cutaway sections. Now she could hear more clearly, and she recognized Harley Sprague's voice saying, "I don't know. I thought I'd made headway with her. I really did. Now there's this ridiculous shirt like . . . like a defiant flag."

How could a shirt be a flag?

"You'll have to deal with her." This was Mr. Leeward talking. What was he doing with Mr. Sprague inside Gramary's buses? "After this witch thing, I better not get involved. You know, I can't figure out why she's cutting all the struts away here. I can't find any plan or drawing that would show us what she's up to." His voice came and went as he turned and poked around.

"Isn't it a safety hazard?" Mr. Sprague asked. "Couldn't you selectmen stop it for that?"

"I doubt it. Not while people are unstepping masts on the wharf and hauling engines over to the machine shop. We'd have a whole lot of people get their backs up if we tried that."

Merkka grabbed the window edge and pulled herself up so that she could see just the tops of the two men.

"So," declared Mr. Sprague, "we're no wiser."

"It was worth a try, though. Soon as I heard that Bev was

leaving the kid with Ruth, it seemed like a chance in a million to have a look around."

The two men headed for the door. Merkka crouched down and grabbed Jet. She could still hear them talking, puzzling over the buses and what possible plans Gramary had for them. Then Mr. Sprague mentioned the shirt again, this time with grudging admiration. "She's really clever, you know. She had me fooled. It's too bad she hasn't some harmless outlet for all that creative energy."

"She still does the odd welding job for the old-timers," Mr. Leeward told him. "Of course, they'll none of them hear a word against her. The trouble with Mary Weir is she don't care what the rest of us think."

"Well," said Mr. Sprague, "you weren't that far off calling her a witch. Not that I condone name-calling. It's the way people used to deal with troublesome old women." Merkka heard him laugh. "Those were terrible, brutal times, but I have the least bit of sympathy for the witch hunters if they were up against women like Mary Weir. She's . . ." The voice faded as he turned toward Water Street.

Merkka waited awhile before releasing Jet. The rain made a terrific racket on the buses. The shirt rattled and clanged in the wind. The voices seemed unreal now that they were gone. Had she imagined all that talk about witches? These were grown-up men. What were they thinking of? Didn't they even feel sneaky coming down here like this?

When she stood up, she could see them stop again. They were looking back at Gramary's yard, still talking. They were looking at the shirt. "It's sculpture!" she wanted to shout at Mr. Sprague. At that moment she thought of the poem about the old cars in Maine. Forget blue skies and gray skies. She would practice writing carefully. She would let Ben be the . . . the . . . She had forgotten the word for the person who does the drawing. Ben would be the artist, and she was the word person. She had a project for Ledgeport Appreciation Day.

CHAPTER 16:

Signs of War

A really bad storm gets us from above as well as from below. The ceiling is so stained that sometimes we don't notice the leaks until they begin to run down the walls and splash on the floor. Mom always minds the leaks more than anyone else, but for some reason they don't bother me very much. Maybe it's because I can see where they come from and where they're going. I'm not afraid of a little rain.

The soup pot in front of the living room window had to be emptied before bedtime so that it wouldn't overflow during the night. Usually Gramary saw to it. Tonight Mom sat downstairs with the television on so that she would stay awake to empty the pot. She told Merkka she was waiting up in case Dad came home.

Merkka woke to the pinging of the rain in the pot downstairs and laughter in her parents' room. She jumped out of bed and stood outside their door calling softly until Mom heard her and told her to come in.

Dad, half-dressed, was sitting on the edge of the bed. He was telling Mom about Grace Island, about Gramary and Charlie Budge. "They've got those things all over the place," he said. "I guess Ma's been making them for weeks and stashing them."

"What things?" Merkka asked.

"Junk," said Mom.

"Not exactly junk," Dad explained. "See, Suzy Cope told Ma she had to come back to Grace Island after the operation because she was afraid she might die without ever seeing all her favorite things again. Had to come back for sea urchins and sand dollars and seals and osprey. So Ma made them all. There's this giant sand dollar up against Suzy's kitchen window. Made from the cover of a fifty-gallon oil drum. And you'd never guess what we had to take out to the wreck. Ma made me back right up to it, waited till high tide so she could lash the thing down about where the dog was. A mite touchy out there. When I asked her why we were risking our boat for it, she says, "To catch someone's eye." Then she says, "To catch someone. It's a watchdog.""

"A watchdog!" Merkka exclaimed.

"That's what she called it. Lord knows what Suzy will make of the thing."

Dad didn't have long to wait to find out, because two days later Mrs. Cope arrived in Ledgeport. It was afternoon. Merkka and Ben were helping clean bait off the *Little Mary* when Mrs. Cope called down from the wharf. Dad left the children and climbed up the ladder to talk with her. When she found out that both Gramary and Charlie Budge were already on the island, she asked Dad to take her out there.

He brought the *Little Mary* around to Ingalls' float so that Mrs. Cope could use the ramp. It was slow going on her shiny metal crutches. Norm Gray said they'd better carry her. Mrs. Cope said she could get in and out of the boat under her own steam. Everyone stood around to watch her trying to edge her way down the steep incline.

"It's Charlie's fault," she complained. "If his boat were here, he could bring it right up on the beach for me."

"I doubt that," Ed Ingalls replied. "Not if he planned to ship out again."

Merkka thought Ed was brave to disagree with Mrs. Cope.

Mrs. Cope glared up at him, but before she could say anything more, Dad said, "Better let us carry you, Suzy."

She looked them over and selected with care. "You," she said, pointing to Spike. "And Sam. But bear in mind the leg can't bend." She pulled off her hat, looked around, and ordered Merkka to hold onto it. "And if it's soiled or mashed," she threatened, "you'll be sorry."

Merkka went forward to receive the hat, not straw like Mrs. Cope's summer ones, but made of some soft material that dented at the slightest touch.

Spike and Dad had to reverse positions before they could begin the slow descent.

"No hurry," Mrs. Cope reminded them needlessly as they inched along, their feet sliding from one cleat to the next.

They were midway when Russell Leeward burst on the scene. He didn't stop to see what Spike and Dad were carrying. He just caught sight of Dad's back, took note of the *Little Mary* snubbed to the float below, and yelled, "Sam, you're going to have to do something about your mother."

"Just a minute," Dad answered. His voice sounded muffled.

"Put that down," Mr. Leeward shouted, "and listen to me."

Dad and Spike actually hesitated, as if they were considering Mr. Leeward's order.

Mrs. Cope's voice rose up from between them. "Carry on!"

The two men moved on down the ramp. Mr. Leeward craned at them and their burden, his expression turning from rage to perplexity to disbelief. Spike, landing first, spread his legs to take on more of Mrs. Cope. He swayed. Dad stepped down heavily, shifting the weight to balance himself. He called Merkka down to position the tire he'd put in the boat for Mrs. Cope to sit on. Merkka plunged the hat on her head, became aware of Mrs. Cope's indignant gaze, and stuck the hat between her legs while she dragged the tire closer to the bulkhead. Spike and Dad carried Mrs. Cope into the boat and set her down with support for her back. Then they stood on either side of her, their arms still out the way people do who prop things up they're not sure will stay.

Mrs. Cope waved them aside. She looked up at Russell Leeward. "What has Mary done," she asked him, "that's so dreadful you wanted Sam to drop me for it?"

"I didn't . . . couldn't see." Mr. Leeward turned from her to Ed and Norm. Then he summoned up his anger and declared hotly, "She tried to lay a curse on us. I know it's her. She's the only one that could do it. So help me."

"Adding," muttered Mrs. Cope, "to her already considerable accomplishments."

"What?"

"We are in her debt," Mrs. Cope remarked in full voice.

"You mean you know about this?" Mr. Leeward's hand shot out. Something glinted redly. Everyone stared at it. Everyone waited for him to explain.

"What's the problem, Russ?" Dad inquired.

"She put this there. Secretly. Just like what she put out there on the wreck."

Mrs. Cope tried to twist around. "Like what?"

"Mary made something," Mr. Leeward told her. "I don't know what you'd call it, but she put it on the wreck where the dog was."

"So you noticed it," Dad exclaimed. "Ma was hoping you would."

"Harley Sprague saw it. From his living room window. He told me about it. Of course I knew it was her. She's fighting everything we're trying to do here in Ledgeport to upgrade . . . upgrade. . . . Sam, she can't go around like this. She can't."

"There's nothing Sam can do now," Mrs. Cope put in. "Whatever you think Mary's done is done. Meanwhile I'm waiting for Sam to take me out to the island. I'm just out of the hospital and it's been a grueling day already."

"It's not what I *think* she's done," Russell Leeward sputtered. "I'm talking about what she's actually gone and done. To me and my family. It's no joke when people make little fighter planes and aim them at your house."

"Let's see." Ed Ingalls pulled back and squinted at the object in Mr. Leeward's hand. "Looks like a bird to me."

"It's a symbol," Mr. Leeward retorted. "Harley Sprague said so. A spite . . . a spite-thing. That red on it? That's supposed to be blood."

"It looks from here," Mrs. Cope remarked, "like a model. Rather nice."

"That's it," Mr. Leeward agreed. "A model. That's what those symbols are."

Merkka said, "It's a tern."

"A symbol stands for something," Mr. Leeward went on. "They made models of people in the old days and stuck pins in them."

Merkka said, "It was for Darleen. Her birthday present."

"Darleen? What kind of present is that for a girl? It's got blood on it. All the other presents were nice."

"I know," said Merkka. "I knew that, and I didn't know what to do, so I bought her bubble gum instead."

"Well," said Mr. Leeward as he lowered the tern and stepped back from the group at the edge of the wharf, "it could easily be taken for a fighter plane. It wasn't right. Harley Sprague said—"

"Harley thought that bird was a fighter plane?" Mrs. Cope demanded.

"Well, yes. From my description. And who would ever make a tern red like this. There is no such bird."

"It's in the eye of the beholder," Mrs. Cope told him. Then she added to Dad, "Can we get up close to the wreck on our way out? I want to see the other thing Mary left there. And I think we should move along now. My knee is beginning to object to this position."

"Just tell Mary to lay off," Mr. Leeward shouted as Dad started up the engine.

"He's really afraid of her," Mrs. Cope murmured. The *Little Mary* chugged slowly out of the harbor. "Russell's all fussed up," she said. "What's he up to, Sam?"

Dad steered around the end of the breakwater and inside the monument. "Can't get much closer," he told Mrs. Cope. "Tide's too low."

They all stared at the model dog on the wreck. If you didn't know it was supposed to be a watchdog, you might easily take it for a seal. It was full and curved and sleek; it seemed to have just turned its head. Watching.

Looking at it, Merkka forgot that it was made from a fender. Watchdog, she thought. That was what she saw.

Dad said, "Russell's after the waterfront, I think."

Mrs. Cope nodded. "I see."

They were heading out now, the wreck and its watchdog astern. Mrs. Cope, who sat facing aft, seemed to brood over what she had seen and heard. Finally she spoke as if finishing a thought. "Russell may be right about Mary." Mrs. Cope nodded to herself as she smoothed her skirt and held it down from the wind. "One way or another," she concluded, "it looks as though Mary's declared war."

Merkka, clutching the battered hat, remained silent. She could see Mrs. Cope's gaunt face brighten with the thought.

CHAPTER 17:

If I Had an Island

You have to listen hard to pick up the pieces grown-ups leave out of what they tell you. Because I'm older than Ben, I've heard more. I know that when Dad mentions hard times from when he was little, he's really talking about the years after Grampa couldn't go lobster fishing anymore and Gramary had to keep it up as best she could. Uncle Henry has a scar on his cheek from when he was a baby and fell against the exhaust pipe and got burned. Gramary took him and Dad lobster fishing to keep them out of Grampa's way. I know now that when Grampa fell into the harbor and drowned he was already very sick and probably drunk, but it took a long time for me to understand that. I think grown-ups should tell us the whole truth. But whenever I hear Dad leaving things out of what he tells Ben, I pretend that I believe all of it. I don't know why that is.

Gramary hardly spoke to Mrs. Cope until she was comfortably settled on her living room couch. By then, Dad had gone back to the boat, but Merkka and Ben hung around to watch and listen.

Gramary stood over Mrs. Cope. "If you had any sense you would have rented a wheelchair for getting around."

Mrs. Cope was trying to punch her hat into shape. She didn't even look up. "I don't like wheelchairs."

"They're not to like," Gramary informed her. "They're useful when you need them."

"I'll be just fine," Mrs. Cope told her. "What's that great big sand dollar doing in the kitchen?"

"Ninety-three years old. You should've brought a nurse."

"I didn't want to. I like privacy. You made that sand dollar, Mary. And this starfish. What else is there? Is that a sea urchin over by the wood carrier?" Mrs. Cope began to laugh. "It's got nails sticking out all over it."

"I ran out of used nails, and I won't waste new ones. I'll get around to finishing it eventually. As for privacy, you won't have any, because I'm staying here for the time being. Did you ever think I might have work of my own to do? Three days already, out here, putting up with Charlie and fixing ramps and duck-walks and that."

Charlie, who was leaning against the farthest wall, said, "I built you a real nice stool, Suzy. You can sit at the kitchen sink and pump water. We did all kinds of things, Mary and me."

Mrs. Cope looked across the room at him and smiled. "Thank you, Charlie. But I've no intention of imposing on Mary. She can go home with Sam and the kids. Or with you. I don't need anyone."

Gramary swept up Mrs. Cope's hat and stomped into the kitchen.

Charlie straightened. "Mary didn't mean you'd imposed. She's just had a lot on her mind lately, and she's worried—"

"Don't speak for me, Charlie Budge," Gramary called from

the kitchen. "I meant every word. And I'm a lousy nurse too. As Dayle could have told you."

"He did," Mrs. Cope snapped back. "He complained about you all the time."

Merkka grabbed Ben's sleeve. She had to drag him away before he heard any more.

"Why did you do that?" he demanded crossly. "I wanted to stay and listen." He kicked a stone as they trudged down the path.

"It wasn't nice," Merkka told him. She felt strange as soon as she said it, as if someone else had spoken for her.

Dad showed them he was anxious to be off by starting the engine the minute he saw them coming. Almost at once they were heading for home.

"Did Grampa really complain about Gramary?" Ben asked him.

Dad didn't answer right away. Then he said slowly, "Grampa was sick a long time. Hurting."

"Is Mrs. Cope hurting?"

Merkka said, "They were arguing."

Dad beckoned Ben to the wheel so that he could help steer the boat. Then he said, "Mrs. Cope may be hurting some. But she and Ma, they just go at each other like that. Except in hard times, like when Mr. Cope died. Then Mrs. Cope only wanted Gramary with her."

Ben asked, "What about when Grampa died?"

"That was hard times too," Dad said. "Your grandmother tried to make extra money welding, but mostly she mended things for friends, so she never charged enough. Of course in the summer time she had the Grace Island laundry. Used to be lots of it then. Things were always better in the summer, meaner in the winter."

"Did Grampa die in the summer or the winter?"

Dad frowned a memory into place. Merkka stared at Ben's small hands on the wheel and Dad's big ones beside him. The

Little Mary jogged and slapped over the chop, gulls crisscrossing in its wake. Was Dad remembering a time when he stood at the wheel in front of his father? Probably it was Gramary's hands he recalled beside his own, not Grampa's.

"It was fall," Dad said. "Later than this, close to Thanksgiving. Your grandma and us boys were coming in one day, squalls popping all around us. Your grandpa tried to come down to the float to meet us. We saw him. We saw him stop on the ramp like he'd forgotten something. Then he fell down. Down and into the harbor. We couldn't get to him right off, but it wouldn't have made a difference. It was a blood vessel burst. It was merciful."

Merkka couldn't imagine seeing your own father falling down drunk, dead, drowned. She pressed up against Dad, just to feel the warmth and strength of him standing with Ben at the wheel.

They watched the town of Ledgeport come into view. Merkka thought she could see Jet waiting for them at the wharf. Watching. Watch dog. She cast a look at the wreck, which hardly showed now. The watch dog was partly submerged.

"Tide's coming," she said.

Dad chuckled. "Just like Mrs. Cope to come at dead low and expect to be delivered down the ramp. She's some sure of herself."

"And of you," Merkka pointed out. "You and Spike."

Dad laughed. "That's true. And of Gramary and Charlie."

Merkka said, "If I owned an island, I'd paint the house lavender."

Ben said, "If I owned an island, I'd make a house that looked like a weapons carrier."

Dad said, "If I owned an island, I'd sell it and buy a new boat."

"What would you name it?" Merkka wanted to know.

"Little Mary," Dad declared. "That's the only name."

Merkka gave a sigh. "Only we don't own an island. And if we did and sold it, Mom would buy a house on the mainland. In town."

"I know," said Dad. "I know that."

Merkka knew they were no longer playing "If I had an island." They were talking about the waterfront and the part of it Gramary owned.

"And would you like that, Little Mary?" Dad asked her.

This was important. "Yes," she breathed. "Yes."

Dad didn't say any more. It was time to go up forward with the bowline. Jet, wriggling with joy, jumped aboard and got in Merkka's way. The *Little Mary* churned up water, because Dad put her in reverse. Merkka could feel the line quiver as she snubbed it down and made it fast.

CHAPTER 18:

Old Black Magic

*When Gramary is working hard, she sings old songs
and hymns. Especially when she comes to the end of a
job or solves some problem. Then she sings loud enough
for a whole church choir. You wouldn't want just
anyone to hear her then, not if the words are about
finding her thrill on Blueberry Hill. With Charlie Budge,
it's mostly whistling, so you can't mind too much. Only
sometimes when the two of them get together they start
belting out those old lines for all the town to hear. The
only thing to do is stay as far away from them as you
can.*

It was soon clear that the word had spread about the Witch of
the Waterfront and her spite things. It was a joke, of course.
Even the wharf crowd picked it up and played with it.

"No wonder Charlie's always whistling 'Black Magic,'"
Merkka heard Norm saying to the others. "He's still carrying
the torch for her, isn't he?"

Charlie carrying Gramary's welding torch? Merkka waited until she found Ed Ingalls alone to ask him about that.

"Some scraps over there for your grandmother," he remarked, nodding at fine coils he'd slivered off a steel coupling. Merkka started to gather them up. "Careful now. They're wicked sharp." He left his drill press and kicked through rubbish until he came across a small cardboard carton. "Set them in here so's you don't cut yourself."

The coils were shiny and vicious-looking. "Did Charlie Budge used to work for Gramary?" Merkka asked.

Ed Ingalls looked all around, as if to confirm that they were alone. Then he said, "You'll have to ask Charlie about that. Or Mary."

"Is it a secret?"

"Well, now . . ." Ed's voice trailed off like the beginning of a story, but he didn't go on.

"I can't ask them. They're still out taking care of Mrs. Cope."

Ed Ingalls told Merkka to be careful again. "I wouldn't call it secret," he said. "Not if you've been around awhile."

"I've been around all my life," she responded.

That brought a smile, then a sort of cough. "I guess I had something else in mind. A few more years than you've got on you. You know, Mary and I were in school together."

"You were?" It was hard to tell ages of grown-ups.

"And she'd stand here talking with my father just the way you are with me."

"What did she talk about?"

"Goodness knows. Boats. Fishing. She was keen to design things. My father made boats."

"And was Charlie Budge in school with you too?"

"Charlie was younger, though he hung around a lot. Always hustling to catch up to the rest of us. Figuring shortcuts, just like he does now."

They were a long way from talking about secrets now. They were far from where Merkka had intended to come, and she knew that was no accident. Ed Ingalls had avoided answering her question.

When Merkka put the carton of steel shavings in Gramary's buses, she took a moment to look around. Dad had removed the metal shirt from the line and propped it on one of the remaining bus seats. It looked funny that way because it still had the fullness of wind blowing through it, wrinkles and all. When Gramary had left suddenly to help get the island ready for Mrs. Cope, she had been dismantling the bracing for the bus roofs. Some of it was already cut away, and her acetylene torch looked as though she had just set it down. Carrying the torch, thought Merkka, wondering again. What kind of job would that have been? It was confusing, because she knew that Gramary and Charlie did work together sometimes, like on Grace Island.

A few other things caught Merkka's eye. One of Ben's trucks, for instance. It had lost its tiny steering wheel and its hood that opened up. Gramary must have rescued it when Mom threw it out.

Merkka crawled between a sheet of plywood and some expanded metal mesh to retrieve the truck from where Gramary had set it out of her way. Her fixing had changed it. Merkka saw that the new steering wheel was shaped like a tiny tongue. The front of the truck had become the face of an animal, something like a squirrel. If you set it up on end, the rear wheels became haunches and the front wheels looked like curved forepaws. The windshield was the brow and eyes, the new hood a snout. Creepy! Merkka let out a cry and dropped the thing. When it landed on its crouched legs, they were wheels again with funny fenders, not legs anymore. It was just one of Gramary's weird inventions.

It reminded Merkka of the weapons carrier Ben had drawn to go with the poem she had copied out. It was like Gramary's real one, with bits of this and parts of that from every imaginable model of truck and tractor. It was a wonderful picture, but not what you'd call normal. Mulling all of this, Merkka left the buses.

Mom was home already. She was home a lot more now. It felt strange. With Gramary gone, everything was different. Mom was throwing clothes in a heap as if she were angry at them. She paused long enough to tell Merkka the kitchen floor was wet and to take off her shoes.

Merkka leaned against Dad's heavy jacket. It slipped from the hook.

"I just finished telling you the floor's washed. Pick that up."

Merkka picked it up, but she couldn't get it to stay on the hook, so she held it.

Mom crossed the kitchen on tiptoe and hung up Dad's jacket. She said, "If I'm going to have to stay home, it will at least look presentable."

"Won't we ever move to the new house?"

Mom's shoulders sagged. "I don't know." Her voice dropped. "Honestly, Merkka, there's no telling. Not if your grandmother decides to teach Russ Leeward a lesson."

"Mr. Leeward told me I could help. I don't know how."

"Oh, hon." Mom turned away and went back to her sorting. "I don't know how either." Wheeling around, she held up a skirt. "We may just have to make the best of this place." She tossed the skirt on the heap.

"Are you throwing that away?" cried Merkka. "It's almost new."

"Not throwing," Mom said. "Just making room for some other things."

"Did you go shopping?" Merkka meant, *Without me?* Going to the mall off Route 1 was a rare adventure.

Mom said no, she hadn't been anywhere, not in a long time. Her voice took on the bite it so often had these days. "No shopping. I'm finished at work now. I don't know when I'll be making money again. Or where."

Merkka said, "Oh."

"Maybe your grandmother will decide to let us put a snack bar here, and then we'll use our own lobsters and won't have to ship them. We'll set our own prices, then."

That sounded wonderful. "And we'll live in the Haskell Gray house," Merkka chimed in.

"Maybe," Mom said, letting their dreams of patios and lavender and yellow rooms draw them close for a moment.

When Merkka came home from school the next day, Mom said, "I saw Russ Leeward today, and he said to make sure you do something special for the contest. He said if you win, that could show Mary how important it is for you kids."

"I did something already," Merkka told her. "With Ben. He drew a picture and I copied a poem."

"That's good," Mom exclaimed. "That's just what Russ had in mind."

"I don't think so," Merkka murmured.

"Sure it is. He said a little child shall lead them."

"I'm not little," objected Merkka.

"It's a saying. It's out of the Bible. Show me what you did, hon."

Merkka stalled. "It might be in school. It might not work, because Ben's thing should be in the under-six group and mine belongs in the nine-to-thirteen group."

She took Jet out to the Budge place to water the sheep. They were eating down the bleached pasture, but they looked peaceful spread out on the slope with the dark bay behind them glinting in the crisp October air. Every rock and island seemed outlined in black penciling and fringed in white. The wind tore at the top of each wavelet. You could see flecks of spume all the way to the horizon.

There ought to be a way of painting all of it in words, Merkka thought. They would be a poem, the kind that Mr. Leeward had in mind. But how did he know what the judge would like? How could he be sure that she would win and show Gramary what must be done?

Words. What she needed was another kind of magic word, not the kind that sent Jet scooting around behind the sheep, but the kind Lucy's father had mentioned. Jet was like the wind today, hurling himself this way and that. Merkka could tell that he was eager to be off and doing something, driving those sheep somewhere, anywhere. When she called him to her, he fixed her with a pleading look.

They started back home. In her mind Merkka began collecting words that rhymed, like blue and view, like hull and gull. No, not hull. Mr. Leeward had something pretty in mind. Yacht, for instance. Yacht and pot, rot, hot. Well, then, sail. He'd like something about a sail. And gale? Or whale.

By the time she reached home she had some rhymes. She didn't have a poem.

"Tell me again what Mr. Leeward likes," she asked her mother.

Mom sighed. "I don't know. Go up to the Variety Store. Look at the greeting cards. They've got poems in them."

Merkka left Jet with Ben. She went to the Variety Store. Marilyn behind the counter wouldn't let her unwrap anything, but there were two cards that had boat pictures and poems inside. One said, "Home is the sailor, home from the sea; fond are the wishes you have from me." The other one said, "All the seas may ebb and flow, as men have learned from long ago, but love, true love, will 'ere abide, more constant than the fickle tide." These poems were like valentines. They didn't paint a picture with words.

Merkka stumped up to Lucy's house. Lucy, who had finished her model, thought it was pretty late to be starting a new project, but she helped find some poetry books to look through. Since they couldn't find the exact ones Mr. Starobin had shown Merkka, they flipped through other ones looking for seashore and boat words. Most of the poems were complicated and about things they didn't understand.

Lucy's brother, Jay, came home from high school and suggested they think of songs instead.

The two girls sat on the floor and sang, "I've been working on the railroad."

"Not about trains."

They sang, "Row, row, row your boat."

"I won't help if you act dumb," he told them.

Merkka said, "We were trying to find a poem that would show us how."

"Show *you* how," corrected Lucy.

Jay said, "Just a minute," went into the kitchen, and returned with a handful of cookies. "Okay," he said. "Okay, now think about a certain time of day and all the things you see then."

Merkka tried to think of a time. Nothing came.

"Like just before it gets dark," he prompted. "Lots of poems are about sunsets and stuff. Think of your dad coming into the harbor just before dark."

"He's usually home before that. He leaves in the dark."

"Whatever." Jay had had enough. "Keep thinking. It'll come to you."

On her way home Merkka detoured past the Haskell Gray house. It had a For Sale sign out front. She stood looking up at the upstairs windows, imagining herself in the yellow room. The yellow turned to lavender, and she was inside that color, gazing out at a scrap of water and the end of the town wharf. Word pictures began to form. Even as she turned onto Landing Road and headed down to Water Street, the whispered words came.

> I see wharf and moorings and boats,
> I see pilings, I see floats.
> Farther off in watery space,
> I see islands, Tinkers and Grace.
> I see lobsters, I see clams,

I see sheep and I see lambs.
I see Ledgeport every day,
the greatest town in every way.

"It's like a cheer," said Miss Guarino when Merkka showed it to her the next day. "You might want to tone it down a little."

"Couldn't I just call it a cheer," Merkka asked, "and leave it the way it is?"

"Then you'd better add, 'Rah! Rah! Rah!'"

Looking up at Miss Guarino, Merkka realized that was meant to be funny. But later she began to worry about the cheer. She ended up adding two more lines.

Ledgeport shining like a star,
Ledgeport! Ledgeport! Rah, Rah, Rah!

"It doesn't rhyme," said Lucy.

"You won't notice when you're shouting it," Merkka assured her. Only she couldn't get rid of the sinking feeling when she handed it in to Miss Guarino. It just made the entry deadline.

CHAPTER 19:

Spending Sheep

*It seems as though once people get talking about witches
and spells and magic the thoughts about those things
hang around for a while. Maybe it's because of
Halloween coming at the end of October. Maybe it just
seemed that way to me, because Ledgeport Appreciation
Day was set for the day after Halloween. It was hard to
separate the two; they went together like trick and
treat.*

"When is Gramary coming home?" Merkka asked Mom. The
sheep were getting restless now that their grass was eaten
down. "We need hay. Gramary knows what to do about it."

"Don't expect me to pay good money for hay," Mom declared.

Merkka found Dad mending traps. "Are you going to Grace
Island soon?"

He said he would be taking out groceries tomorrow. Merkka
asked him to tell Gramary the sheep were hungry.

The next afternoon, when the *Little Mary* came into view in the outer harbor, Merkka ran down to meet Dad. He told her that Gramary had said to call Mr. Brackett and ask him to bring over some hay. But first Merkka would have to clear a space in the shed at the end of Charlie's barn.

So Merkka took off for Limeburner Point and worked until dark getting the shed ready for Mr. Brackett. That night she called him, and he promised to come tomorrow after school. But it was only when she heard his truck rattling onto the dirt driveway that it occurred to her that he had probably timed his delivery so that she would be there to pay him for the hay. She made Jet stand way back out of the way.

"Where to?" Mr. Brackett shouted out the cab window.

She pointed to the end of the barn. He had to stop short of the shed because the hay was piled higher than the shed roof.

Merkka called up to him. "Wait, Mr. Brackett. I don't have any money."

Mr. Brackett climbed onto the back load and picked up a bale. It dropped neatly at the rear of the shed. Another followed.

"I can't pay you," she told him.

With the next bale poised, Mr. Brackett looked down at her. "You better keep count," he said. "This is bale number three."

"Three," she agreed, wondering how much each bale was going to cost.

Thirty bales in all were stacked in Charlie's shed. Then Mr. Brackett looked around and asked Merkka how she was going to get the hay to the sheep.

Merkka hadn't considered that. "Can't I drag each bale?"

Mr. Brackett loaded two back onto his truck and told her to climb up beside them. After he drove to the pasture gate, he left one bale for tomorrow and threw the other into the field. He taught her to use Jet to keep the sheep away while she spread it in neat piles so little of it would be wasted. Jet was ecstatic at having a job to do for Mr. Brackett. He stared the sheep down and backed them off and then stood there, his ears erect, his eyes keeping them at a distance until Mr. Brackett called him off.

"I miss this guy," Mr. Brackett said when Jet came bounding over to him. "Toby," said Mr. Brackett as Jet looked up at him.

Merkka blurted, "Take him back then." That would keep Jet out of Charlie's clutches. "He wants to work so bad, and I don't know what to do for him."

"No." Mr. Brackett shook his head. "Bobby sold him to Charlie."

"Charlie Budge went and left him for dead. He nearly drowned."

"It's his dog now," Mr. Brackett told her.

Merkka drew a breath. "Even if he threw him into the water?"

"Charlie? What kind of thing is that to say? Your grandmother would never stand for you saying such a thing."

"It's true," Merkka insisted weakly. If only she could unsay those words. She should have realized that no grown-up would believe her. "Anyway," she mumbled, trying to change the subject, "Gramary will pay for the hay when she comes home."

Mr. Brackett scowled at her. He walked stiffly to the truck. "Mary and I have been helping each other out a good many years."

Merkka followed him, her face aflame.

"I've been thinking of bringing over some repair work for her," he went on. "I'll leave it in the yard tomorrow."

"Is it very big?" Merkka asked anxiously. "Because if it is, there might not be room for it until after Halloween."

"It's my old pinwheel rake," Mr. Brackett said. "I'm getting a new mower-conditioner, and I'm selling the rake as soon as I get them broken tines welded."

"A big rake for behind the tractor?" Merkka pressed.

Mr. Brackett turned and looked at her. "I'll just bring the disks that need fixing. Will that do?"

Merkka nodded gratefully. Those disks, whatever they were, couldn't be as big as a whole hay rake.

"And tell your grandmother I'll take them ram lambs before they get all the ewes bred. The ram lambs ought to pay for your winter hay. You can tell her that; or tell Charlie," he added pointedly.

Merkka nodded again. He wasn't exactly forgetting what she'd said, but he didn't sound angry anymore. She dared to tell him, "Not the speckled lamb. That one's my brother's."

He told her he would give her and the dog a lift home; it wasn't good to be out on the road at dusk, especially with a black dog. And when she and Jet were inside the cab with him, he looked them over slowly and allowed that he couldn't feel too bad about losing the dog when it seemed to have found itself such a good friend. He nodded at her as he spoke. Maybe he meant that Jet might be all right with her after all. She rode home with her fingers buried in Jet's soft, warm undercoat.

The following morning, when Darleen Leeward stopped her in the hall and told her to go to Mr. Leeward's office after school, Merkka's first thought was that there was some important message about the Haskell Gray house. But when Mrs. Leeward met her at the office door and told her to go straight up the hill to Mr. Sprague, Merkka was mystified. Of course Mr. Leeward didn't need to send messages about the house to Mom, not when Mom and Mrs. Leeward were such good friends.

"Why didn't Darleen just tell me that?" Merkka asked.

"We didn't want anyone to know," Mrs. Leeward told her.

Merkka hesitated. There seemed to be some kind of grown-up secret that she ought to know about.

"Just go," Mrs. Leeward said. She sounded as though she wanted to be rid of Merkka as quickly as possible. "You'll be glad you did," she promised.

Merkka paused along the steep, curving road to Mr. Sprague's house to glance down over the waterfront. She couldn't see Gramary's buses from here, but she recalled how they stood dead center in the view from Mr. Sprague's retaining wall.

Mr. Sprague took Merkka into the book-lined study where she couldn't help but notice all the contest entries stacked and spread out on tables and on the floor. There were piles of papers; there were wood carvings and afghans and a whole collection of stitched and painted covers for *TV Guides*. Somewhere among all those things was the poem she had copied and Ben's drawing for it.

Mr. Sprague said, "Your little brother is quite an artist."

Merkka waited. It helped to look around the edges of the room. She caught sight of Lucy's model of the town green on the floor beside a globe.

"We would like to recognize his talent," Mr. Sprague went on. "The problem is his picture mocks everything this contest stands for."

"Mocks," repeated Merkka, trying to understand.

"What I'm trying to say is that if you could submit something more appropriate, we would accept a late entry."

"You want him to draw something else?"

"Something, ah, positive. Like your cheer," he added with an encouraging smile.

"But that's all he draws," Merkka protested.

"He's never drawn a picture of your father's boat or sea gulls and sails on the water?"

"I don't think so. He likes cars and tractors and trucks." She managed not to mention buses.

Mr. Sprague sighed. Then he said, "I'm sure Mr. Leeward explained that we are hoping, by gentle persuasion, to change your grandmother's mind about her use of the waterfront."

Merkka nodded. "How soon do you have to get the new picture?"

"Right away."

How could Merkka produce something right away when it didn't even exist?

Mr. Sprague said, "It would be a shame for your brother to miss out." He handed her Ben's picture of the weapons carrier and the poem she had copied with such care.

"Do I have to find another poem to copy?"

"Not at all. Your own cheer is fine. You see, I've read everything submitted. I had to in order to select the best ones for the judge. He'll be here tomorrow to collect them, so I must have your brother's new entry as soon as possible. Right after school perhaps?"

He walked her to the door. "I see there's some new litter out in your grandmother's yard," he remarked. "Do you know what she plans to do with it?"

Merkka shook her head. She had no idea what he meant by litter. She took off before he could ask any more impossible questions. As soon as she got home she ran upstairs and shoved the rejected picture and poem in her bureau.

Mom was cross because Mr. Brackett had come by and dumped a bunch of machinery parts out beyond the buses. She poured out her anger to Dad. "How can we get along in town and plan for Ledgeport Appreciation Day when there's all this junk in our backyard?"

"Ma will take care of it," Dad promised. "She'll be home soon."

"She will?" cried Ben. "I'll make her a present."

Merkka tried to draw him aside.

"Stop it. Let go."

"Come upstairs," Merkka whispered.

"No. You hurt me."

"You'll be glad," Merkka informed him. She could hear Mrs. Leeward saying that to her. She didn't think she was glad she had gone up the hill to Mr. Sprague's. "Please," she wheedled, but she couldn't think of a bribe.

"Oh, go upstairs, both of you," snapped Mom.

Glowering, Ben followed Merkka to their room.

"Now," she said brightly, "I'll tell you what you can do that will be really good. You can make a picture of sea gulls and sails."

"Of what?"

"Sea gulls—"

"No," he said.

"You have to, Ben. It's important."

"Why?"

"Because our car poem and picture were wrong."

"How do you know?"

"I just do. But you can have another chance. Because it was my fault. You have a chance to win if you hurry up and do it right now."

Ben didn't look cooperative, so she added with a rush, "You can give Gramary the car picture and the poem. That'll be the present for her coming home."

"No, I can't," he said. "We gave it to the contest."

"I think we can get it back," she said cautiously, "if you put in a new one instead."

"No. I like that one. It's my best picture."

"Listen, Ben," she said desperately, "if you do a picture of gulls and sails, I'll give you one of my sheep."

"You already gave me one."

"I'll give you another. And if they have babies, you'll have three sheep or even four."

Ben thought a moment. Then he said, "Sails? Gulls? How do you draw them?"

"I don't know. You're the artist, not me."

He frowned. He reached for a pad of paper. "Merkka," he said, "I really don't want to." But he crouched and began to draw. After a while he tore the sheet off and started over. He took a long time. Merkka saw that he had drawn the bell out in the Narrows. The bell was very good. Above it hovered a sea gull. It looked like a fish with wings. He hadn't done any sails yet.

After supper Merkka bribed Ben with the promise of another

sheep if he would start a brand-new picture. She told him to try scenery this time, islands and stuff like that. By bedtime she had given away three sheep and she had in return five unsatisfactory pictures. Tomorrow she would take them straight to Mr. Sprague on the hill and let him decide which one to show the judge. There was nothing else she could make Ben do.

CHAPTER 20:

Fitting Entries

*It seems to me that most grown-ups have different rules
about what's fair than the rules that Lucy and I go by. I
can't say exactly what that difference is. I just know
that I don't feel like me when I do things the grown-up
way.*

In the morning Merkka forgot to take the pictures with her, so
after school she had to run home to get them. The house was
empty. She remembered that Mom had said she would be up
at the Town Hall all day. Probably Ben was with her. When
Merkka was upstairs fetching the pictures, a sudden impulse
made her retrieve the original poem and illustration that she
had slipped into her bureau drawer. What else? Her eye fell on
Gramary's tern on the windowsill. She snatched that up too.
Then she had to find a bag to hide it in. It wasn't clear to her
what she meant to do with it, but she knew she didn't want
anyone to see her carrying it up Hill Road.

It had started to rain, but Merkka didn't waste any time getting on her foul-weather jacket. She had to be at Mr. Sprague's house before the judge went away with the entries.

She arrived puffing and quite wet at Mr. Sprague's door. He wasn't pleased at having his floor dripped on, but the man with him looked at her with some concern and said, "Don't you have a raincoat?" Then he added, "I'm just leaving. I'll drive you home."

"That's awfully good of you, Ned," said Mr. Sprague as he flipped through Ben's new pictures. "I'm afraid these aren't up to the other."

"Ben drew them last night," Merkka said. "He didn't want to. I made him."

"I hope you didn't twist his arm," said the judge with a smile. He reminded her a little of Mr. Starobin the way he talked to her.

"I did at first," Merkka admitted, "but I didn't mean to. I gave him a sheep to make him try."

"A sheep," the judge remarked. "That's an unusual form of payment."

"It's all I have," Merkka told him. "Of value."

"That would explain it then," he responded.

Mr. Sprague was shaking his head. "Too bad," he muttered, handing the pictures to the judge. "The first one was extraordinary."

"Where is it?" asked the judge.

"Returned," said Mr. Sprague. "It wouldn't have done."

"Here," said Merkka, withdrawing the weapons carrier picture and poem from the bag. She had to take the tern out, too, so that it wouldn't scratch the paper.

The judge had his eye on the tern. He wanted to know where it came from. Merkka told him. Then he looked at the weapons carrier and burst out laughing.

"It goes with this," Merkka told him, slipping the poem up beside the drawing.

"Wonderful," said the judge. He was grinning broadly. "Yes, I know the poem."

"But it's impossible," Mr. Sprague insisted. "You can see that, Ned, can't you? The contest is to uplift, to upgrade the community. We can't have this kind of thing."

"Yes," the judge agreed, "of course. But it is wonderful."

Merkka and the judge ducked low and ran to his car. He produced a towel from the backseat and handed it to her. Then he drove down to Water Street. When he stopped the car, he asked if he could have a look at some of the other things her grandmother had made. Together they ran to the house and through it to the outside steps. Merkka led him down and then around the buses. There were Mr. Brackett's pinwheel disks, four of them, strewn in the open area in front of the bus door. Each disk, painted yellow with an orange hub, was bigger than a car door, the tines sweeping back and then forward like sunflower petals in a turbulent wind.

Inside the buses the rain made such a racket on what remained of the roofs that Merkka and the judge had to shout at each other.

"That hers?" He was pointing to the horseshoe crab Gramary had made from the seat of an old horse-drawn mower.

"Yes."

"And that?" He had seen the shirt. "Really?"

"She hung it on the clothesline."

The judge raised the shirt with care, then set it back. He ran his hands over the sleeves, shook his head, stood back, shook his head again.

"There's something over there," Merkka yelled, pointing toward the plywood. The judge went over to look and pulled out the truck. He threw back his head and laughed. "Does she do this all the time?"

"It depends on how much real work she has."

"Where did she learn how?"

"From the war Grampa was in," Merkka told him. "She was a welder in a shipyard."

The judge set the squirrel truck down. He looked around slowly, his eye lighting on an unfinished model of Norm's dragger and a herring made of hundreds of tiny washers.

"Where is she, your grandmother?"

"On Grace Island. Helping Mrs. Cope, who had an operation on her knee."

"Mrs. Forrest Cope?"

"I think Forrest is her son, but he's grown up."

"When will your grandmother be back?"

"Soon."

"Do you think she'd mind if I borrowed one or two of these?"

"You mean take them away?"

"Only for a day or so."

Merkka knew she had no right to lend anything that belonged to Gramary. She also knew that even if Gramary noticed that one or two things weren't where she left them, she wasn't likely to care. "What do you want them for?" Merkka asked.

The judge pursed his lips. Then he said, "I'd like to look at them some more. In good light. In my gallery."

Merkka thought he said galley. A ship's kitchen seemed a funny place to look at Gramary's things. "I don't know," she said.

"I'd leave a note. I'd leave my name and address and telephone number. And I'd have them back after . . . soon. That is, unless she agreed to sell them to me."

Sell! Merkka wanted to ask Dad or Mom, but she was afraid the judge would go away and then he would never buy anything at all. She said, "There's a watchdog on the wreck too. It might be a seal."

"Where's the wreck?" he asked.

"Out beyond the breakwater."

"I'll look at it next time."

So he would come back. He wanted to. She said, "Was it a good poem, the one about the cars?"

"I think so."

"Then why doesn't Mr. Sprague like it?"

The judge pursed his lips again. Finally he spoke. "Maybe at another time he would. As I understand it, there's a beautification campaign. The poem doesn't exactly fit." With every word the judge grew more halting. Then he broke in on himself. "Did your grandmother submit something to the contest?"

"Gramary?" Couldn't he see that her things were like the car poem? They didn't fit either. Merkka said, "Her stuff is what they're trying to get rid of."

"Gramary," the judge repeated thoughtfully. "How does she come by that name?"

"From when I was too little to say Grandma Mary."

"Ah," said the judge, and he rested his hand on the metal shirt collar.

Merkka helped him carry the shirt and the squirrel and the horseshoe crab to the car. They had to go the long way around to Water Street, stumbling over rollers and cradle parts, their heads turned from the driving rain, but getting soaked anyhow. After the things were in the car, the shirt in the backseat looking like a headless passenger, Merkka offered him the tern as well. "But not to buy," she added. "I already gave one away."

Wiping his own face with the towel, the judge nodded. He put the tern on the seat beside him. He said, "I don't suppose you'd like to enter it."

"I didn't make it."

"For her. For Gramary," he added.

Merkka, half in and half out of the car, gazed at the tern shaped like an S, its beak curved to its chest plumage. The car was packed with boxes and unboxed entries. "Does it fit?" she asked, thinking that if Gramary won a prize, it would be even more convincing than if Merkka or Ben did.

"It's elegant," he told her. "It's fine."

"Would it still be mine?"

"Of course."

"Okay," she told him. "That's okay then."

"Right. You go inside now and get out of those wet clothes. And be sure to tell your Gramary that I've borrowed her things and would be glad to see more."

Merkka said, "Mrs. Cope has lots of Gramary's stuff on the island."

"I'll have to visit her then," he said. "Maybe I'll get someone to take me out and have a look at the watch dog at the same time. Thank you," he added. "Thank you, Merkka." He paused. "Another unusual name. Where does it come from?"

"Finland. Gramary's mother was Finnish. She was the maid on Grace Island until she married Gramary's father. Merkka means Little Mary."

"So there's Grand Mary and Little Mary," he remarked. "Do you take after her?"

Merkka shook her head. "Ben does. Ben's the artist. Gramary says I'm the word person." She couldn't think how to explain that, so she tried to say it another way. "Some words are special, like magic."

His eyebrows shot up. "I suppose they are."

Merkka wanted to tell him about the magic words and Jet, but she couldn't go on standing there in the drenching rain. Pulling back and shutting the door, she heard him say one more thing through the closed window. Something about Gramary. Something about looking Gramary up in the dictionary. Puzzled, she stood in the downpour watching him back up, turn, and drive out of Water Street and up Landing Road.

What did he mean? she wondered as she dashed into the house. How could Gramary be in a dictionary when no one outside of Ledgeport had ever heard of her?

CHAPTER 21:

Getting Ready

Another thing that's different about grown-ups. When they tell you a storm's brewing, they may not mean the kind of storm you're thinking of, especially when you live on the waterfront. It's important to know about weather. You don't want to be caught unprepared.

On Saturday when Dad went to fetch Gramary home, he took Merkka and Ben with him. They left in the dark to haul lobster traps before heading over to Grace Island. They also had another carton of supplies for Mrs. Cope.

Dad let Ben throw most of the shorts, the undersized lobsters, back into the water. Merkka, filling bait bags, had one ready for each empty trap. In between, she dug her fingers inside her jacket collar to warm them up. Ben was cold, too, but he didn't seem to notice. Or else he was determined to be like Dad.

Whenever Ben threw a small lobster overboard, Jet lurched as though to follow. Each time, Merkka grabbed his collar and pulled him back. "Don't," she crooned, "don't worry." He swung his head around and dashed his tongue over her face. He trembled as Dad measured another lobster and tossed it back to grow some more. "Don't be afraid," she said as Jet's eyes followed the arc the lobster made overhead before it disappeared into the water.

"He's not afraid," Ben told her. "He wants to chase them."

Merkka didn't argue. If Ben didn't know what Charlie Budge had done to Jet, he wouldn't be able to understand what the dog was feeling.

Dad said, "Maybe you could train him to herd lobsters into the harbor. Drive them right into the boxes to wait for the truck."

"Can we?" asked Ben. "Really?"

Dad stopped the winch, then slowly reversed. For a while he was busy untangling trap lines. By the time they were working again, Ben had forgotten his question.

When they pulled alongside the Grace Island float, Charlie was there whistling through his teeth as he nailed a brace to the ramp rail.

Merkka carried the carton to the house. She made Jet come with her, but didn't dare let him inside. "Stay," she commanded. "Stay away from Charlie," she added as she elbowed open the kitchen door. But when she set down the carton, she couldn't help being drawn as usual to Mrs. Cope's living room. Everywhere lay objects of interest, things to touch like a carved wooden spoon, things to turn upside down in the palm of her hand like a shell or a box. Yet there was no sense of clutter. The living room smelled of balsam fir and old books on the edge of mildew. It held the salt smoke of driftwood cinders, the faint reek of dried herbs and starfish, the nip of cloves packed with hard, green apples from wild trees still bearing in the island woods.

Here and there Merkka recognized things that Gramary had made over the years. On the low, round table a centerpiece made of two iron wagon-wheel hubs could be turned, one within the other, to make slits of light or else to cast a full circle thrown by the flame of the stumpy candle they contained. On the hearth two steel porpoises leaped side by side the way you might see them playing out past Limeburner Point. Here they held logs for Mrs. Cope to pick up without bending too low. And standing on its edge like a platter, a chrome scallop shell gleamed metallically. Merkka remembered when Gramary made it out of a hubcap and Mom said she would never feel right serving off it, knowing what it had been before. Merkka's finger itched to take it down. If only she could gather up some of these things for the judge to look at.

"Your grandmother's on her way down to the boat," Mrs. Cope informed Merkka.

Merkka whipped around. There in the doorway from the kitchen stood Mrs. Cope, a cardigan sweater draped over her shoulders, one sleeve twisted around a crutch. As usual, Mrs. Cope's eyes went straight to Merkka's

Merkka met the gaze. "There's a man who wants to see you," she said.

"Here?"

"No, but he might come."

"Who is he?"

"The judge. Not a judge in a court. For the contest about appreciating Ledgeport."

"What's his name. Does he know me?"

"I think so. His name is Ned."

"You call the judge Ned?"

"I don't call him anything. I told him you had a lot of Gramary's things here. He wants to see them."

"I thought he wanted to see me."

"Yes," said Merkka.

"And Mary's things as well?"

"Yes."

"So what is it you haven't yet told me?" Mrs. Cope demanded.

Merkka almost turned away from that stare. "I entered Gramary's tern in the contest. He told me to," she quickly added. She believed that was true now.

"Without her permission?"

"She wasn't there to ask. It was the deadline. Maybe he didn't tell me to exactly, but he wanted me to."

"I'm too old for this," Mrs. Cope declared.

"Too old for what?" asked Merkka.

"For Mary being discovered. And so, I imagine, is she. Anyway, she's obsessed with that bus thing of hers. It's her war machine." The sweater slipped down onto Mrs. Cope's arms. "Still," she went on, "if this Ned person has any taste, Mary's thing will win. Not Ned Copperthwaite by any chance?"

"I don't know."

Mrs. Cope grunted. "Well, so it's entered. I suspect that the less said about it for now, the better."

Just as Merkka was leaving, Mrs. Cope spoke up again. "Do you think he was serious, this Ned?"

"He was . . ." Merkka paused. "He was excited," she finished.

Mrs. Cope nodded. "Probably is Ned Copperthwaite."

"I let him borrow a few other things. He promised to return them. Do you think he will?"

"He will." Mrs. Cope smiled. "Well, well," she said.

"So you really do know him?"

"Yes. Well, we've met a few times."

Ben came pounding up to the door, his arms full of plastic floats, a Clorox bottle, and a bottomless bucket.

"Get my purse," Mrs. Cope told Merkka. "It's on the little table."

Ben stepped inside, but Mrs. Cope very firmly guided him out again. "I don't need sand and rockweed on the floor."

Merkka came back with Mrs. Cope's purse and watched her take out a nickel and two pennies. Merkka said, "I don't see why you only give a penny when the store gives five cents for every bottle."

Ben stood clutching the beach debris. He didn't meet Mrs. Cope's fierce gaze, which swung from him to Merkka and then into the near distance of the kitchen window. Mrs. Cope said, "See that all this business doesn't go to your head."

"What business?"

"Being your grandmother's agent, or promoter, or whatever you are."

"I'm not being anything," Merkka told her. "I just said that about the bottles because I don't think you should take advantage of Ben because he's afraid of you."

"Quite so," Mrs. Cope agreed. "And when he's ready to speak for himself, I may adjust the payment."

"You know he won't say anything."

"He's heard. Haven't you, Ben? That may be an incentive to him to speak up."

The Clorox bottle was sliding out of Ben's grasp.

"What does that mean?" Merkka said. "Say it so he understands."

"Look it up in the dictionary," Mrs. Cope retorted. "Off you go now, both of you. And help your brother with those things." Mrs. Cope shut the door quietly but firmly after them.

Grabbing the Clorox bottle, Merkka looked around for Jet. What if he'd wandered into the woods? Could she persuade Dad to wait for him to come back? She began to run, leaving Ben struggling with the rest of his beach plastic.

But Jet was already on the float. She could see him now, leaning with happiness against Gramary, his muzzle raised to her hand.

As soon as they were home, everything got back to normal. Gramary pounded away inside the buses and bellowed, "Rocked in the cradle of the deep." She was so intent on finishing her roof work there that she never noticed anything missing.

On Sunday Mom made Merkka and Ben go to a special Sunday School session for all ages. Ben wanted to stay with Gramary and help in the buses, but Mom said that would hurt Mrs. Leeward's feelings. In Sunday School they sang two hymns and then made display signs for items to be sold at the Town Hall. Ben drew cars and buses and the weapons carrier. When he started to trade them to other kids for gum and candy, Mrs. Leeward reminded him sharply that he was in the House of the Lord. She took away all the traded things.

When it was time to go home, Merkka gathered up her courage and spoke to Mrs. Leeward. "Ben didn't know it was wrong to sell pictures, because we were making signs for selling stuff next Saturday. He doesn't see the difference."

Mrs. Leeward thought a moment. Then she nodded and said, "That's all right."

Merkka supposed this was sort of an apology and thought Mrs. Leeward would return what she'd taken, but she didn't.

"I'm never going to that House of the Lord again," Ben informed Gramary at lunch.

Gramary ladled out canned chicken noodle soup. "Boring?"

"Stealing," Ben replied.

Gramary paused, the ladle upraised.

"Not exactly stealing," Merkka corrected. "You see—"

"Stealing!" Ben repeated.

"She apologized," Merkka put in. "It was a mistake."

"I'm never going again," Ben insisted.

Gramary said, "I used to feel that way too. Half the women in the Ladies' Missionary Society felt that way when they were your age."

Merkka tried to picture the members of the Missionary Society as children, but they all came out Gramary-shaped and with white hair and ugly dresses.

Gramary set the pot down and turned to Merkka. "What else happened in Sunday School?"

Merkka told her about the signs and the plans for Halloween weekend.

Gramary said, "I'd better lie low then. Maybe I'll go out to the island."

"No!" Merkka exclaimed. "You can't."

"Whyever not?"

"You might be needed here."

Gramary laughed.

"Anyway, I think Mrs. Cope plans to come to town that day."

Gramary looked astonished. "Suzy Cope?"

Now what? wondered Merkka. How could she keep Gramary around to receive her award? "Well," stammered Merkka, "well, she knows the judge."

"What judge?"

Merkka could feel herself plunging toward disaster, but she couldn't stop. "Some judge that's coming that she knows."

"Odd," remarked Gramary dryly.

Merkka slurped her soup and the conversation petered out.

Everything in school that week was geared to the big celebration ahead. On Monday Miss Guarino talked about town history and town government. When they came to correcting last week's spelling mistakes in their workbooks, Merkka had to use the dictionary. First off she turned to the G's to look for *Gramary*. She couldn't find it, so she asked Miss Guarino for help.

"What word?"

"Gramary," said Merkka.

"Two m's."

Merkka turned page after page. She found grammar, but she didn't want it. "Miss Guarino," she called, "I want Gramary with a y."

Miss Guarino looked up from helping Junior Perkins. "It isn't spelled with a y. There's only grammar or grammatical."

Merkka ran her finger down the grammar words that didn't include Gramary. At the bottom of the page she came to a picture of a fish. No, it was a kind of porpoise called a grampus. She was fascinated. A grampa-type word, but no grandma one.

She closed the dictionary and took her notebook back to her desk and began to write a story about a litter of porpussies. They lived in wave nests with Gramma and Grampus porpuss, rocking all day between the waves and eating sea urchins. At lunchtime Miss Guarino came by to check Merkka's spelling corrections. There weren't any, because she had forgotten about them. Miss Guarino made her stay in from recess to get the work done. A bad way to start this all-important week.

At home Mom hummed and didn't have time to do much about meals and was happy again. Gramary was busy, too, and only stopped work when it was too dark to see properly, even with drop cords and light bulbs dangling everywhere.

It was well after dark when Russell Leeward stopped by to talk about cleaning up the waterfront for next weekend. "We're getting all kinds of publicity on this, big newspapers and the tourist organization and someone doing a magazine story."

Dad said, "They must be expecting quite a show."

"I'm going to tell you, Sam, it takes a lot of work to get them interested. This is the big chance for Ledgeport." Mr. Leeward moved over to the kitchen window and looked out over Gramary's yard. "How are things going down here?" he asked.

Dad shrugged. Anyway, it was too dark to see.

"Harley Sprague thought she'd be all cleaned up by now."

Dad said, "I suppose it depends on what you mean by cleaned up. She's been working real hard there. Except when she was out to Mrs. Cope."

"I was wondering what we might expect come Saturday," Russell Leeward went on.

"She's right there in the front room," Dad told him. "Why don't you go in and ask her?"

Russell Leeward looked startled. "In there?"

"Yes," Gramary called from the sofa, where Jet stretched out alongside her. "You might as well come in and sit down."

Merkka followed Mr. Leeward into the living room. Gramary

nodded him toward the low chair out of the Hudson car and asked him what was on his mind.

"Like I said," he began, "like I told Sam . . ." Was Mr. Leeward hoping that Gramary would help him out? She just sat there with her feet up and her attention on him. "Well, Mary, I expect you know about the big weekend coming up. We're working hard to make it, well, big."

Gramary looked at him politely. Dad came partway in and leaned against the doorjamb. He didn't speak either.

"We don't want trouble," Russell Leeward said.

Gramary boosted herself up on her elbow. "You still speaking for the town?" Jet rolled over onto his back and thumped his tail.

Mr. Leeward looked decidedly uncomfortable over this question. "Well," he said, "you know how it is."

"No," said Gramary flatly. Jet groaned happily as Gramary rubbed his upturned chest.

"Oh, hell, Mary, you do know. You're heading straight for trouble. Harley Sprague would've had you in court by now if I hadn't stepped in." When she made no reply, he plunged on. "Look at it this way then. I showed Beverly a real good buy, the Haskell Gray house. It won't be around much longer, not after this weekend, with Ledgeport on the map. You'll see all the prices going up. Now you're already crowded here. What'll it be like come spring? What I'm trying to say is that I've got a buyer for this place, and Sam could keep the bait shack. And then you could move and have plenty of room for the growing family."

"Russell," Gramary said to him, "I'm not as quick as I used to be. I told Harley Sprague I'd fix things down here, and that's what I'm working at. If there's going to be trouble because I'm too slow, I guess I can handle it. That's all I have to say."

Mr. Leeward made a sound like air seeping out of a balloon. "I'm sorry," he told her. "I'm real sorry for all of you then. These are hard times for people who worked in the plant.

We're trying to bring new money in here, some life and jobs. You've always been liked and respected around here, Mary, but I think people are getting fed up with old folk who get themselves in the way of progress. Well . . ." He stood up. "I tried. I gave it my best shot."

Gramary nodded. "You sure have a way of putting things, Russell. And now I think I'll get myself to bed before you start talking about putting me to sleep."

Mr. Leeward had to wait for Dad to step aside to let him through to the kitchen.

As soon as he was gone, Gramary said, "He sure knows how to get a person's back up."

"What kind of trouble will he make?" asked Merkka.

"Nothing," Dad told her. "Don't worry about it."

Gramary shook her head. "Bev really did like that house, didn't she?"

"Yes," said Dad.

"Did you look at it too?"

"No. Haven't been in it for years and years."

"I saw it," Merkka volunteered. "It was like a house on television or in a magazine. It was all new inside. My room upstairs was yellow." She faltered.

"You liked it too," Gramary said.

"Oh, yes. It was perfect. I'd have my friends come and—"

"Your friends come here," Dad pointed out.

"Only Lucy. I wouldn't let anyone else inside."

"I didn't know that," Gramary declared. "My goodness."

Dad, still leaning, flattened his hands on the wall behind him. How alike they looked that way. It was strange seeing Gramary in part of Dad. Did he look like Grampa too? Merkka glanced at the photo of Grampa as a young sailor during World War II. Someday Ben might look like him and Gramary and Dad and Mom. The young man in the photograph had so smooth a face it was hard to connect him with Dad's looks.

For the first time Merkka doubted that it had ever been

Grampa's face she had seen in the rock pool. What if it were a picture of the future instead? What if it were Dad's face? Or Ben's? But it couldn't have been. Merkka didn't believe in visions of the future any more than she believed in witches. Besides, it had been her own face there in the water, that was all. Or a dream, probably a dream.

CHAPTER 22:

Winners and Losers

When you get going on a project and enter it in a contest, you can't help worrying about whether the judge will see it the way he's supposed to. I mean, even if someone's told you how much he liked your cheer and that you don't need to write anything else, you still can't be perfectly sure it will win. But you have a feeling about it. You really do. You wonder what the prize will be. You already feel proud.

By Friday afternoon pumpkin faces grinned from every porch in Ledgeport and dangled from all the trees around the town green. Cardboard fish were strung on lines across Landing Road. One fish contained Halloween candies. At the end of the festivities on Saturday the children would hurl plastic floats— no stones allowed—at the fish. There would be a scramble for the candy when the laden fish dumped its contents all over the ground and a prize for the marksman who brought it down.

"I might be a markswoman," Lucy said to Merkka as she

pitched pebbles at the bird feeder hanging in the maple tree outside her house.

"We'll stand together," Merkka said. "I'll keep the others from jumping in your way."

People kept glancing out to sea and sniffing the air. The weather would at least hold for the supper on the town green and the awards ceremony. Whether the cardboard fish would make it through Saturday was another question.

Everyone was drawn to the green, where cauldrons of beans already bubbled and fires were started for the lobsters and clams. Tables from the church and the grange were decked with foil-wrapped roasting pans and pie plates. The trick was to scout things out beforehand so that when the long lines formed you could head straight for Blanche Ingalls' apple crisp and Mrs. Bowden's buttermilk doughnuts.

The contest entries were inside the Town Hall. Merkka and Lucy walked through just once, spotted their own things, then pretended not to look at them. The Ladies' Missionary Society had donated the quilt they had been working on for months. They had intended to appliqué a Christmas tree in the center, but had made the design appropriate for Ledgeport appreciation instead by turning it into a sailboat. "We just had to change the angle," Dottie Gray was telling Mrs. Brackett. "And turn it around like." But the sail was green. Merkka decided that if she were judge she would not give a prize to the quilt.

She and Lucy walked over to the grange hall to look at fancy work on sale. There were knitted things and straw dolls in gingham dresses. There was even a bargain corner with secondhand items.

Mom was already selling things. When she caught sight of Merkka, she waved some bills at her and sent her back to the Town Hall to get change from Mrs. Leeward. As Merkka and Lucy were leaving, Ida Billings told them to bring back a chair too. "Your mother shouldn't be standing all this time in her condition," she said.

"What condition?" Lucy asked, following Merkka into the Town Hall again.

Merkka shrugged. "Being out of work makes her upset. It makes her tired."

Only Mom didn't look tired when they returned with change and a chair. She had just found a bargain for herself. She was having a wonderful time.

Darkness folded everyone in Ledgeport onto the green. Older kids grouped at the outer edge, radios blaring, cans popping. Merkka and Lucy stood in line for cider that foamed out of the keg and sloshed over hands and paper cups. They had to stand with their backs to the wind to drink it down. Quivering jack-o'-lanterns swung and dipped and looked through diamond eyes, through squares and slits and gaping mouths, on faces Merkka had seen all her life. Probably the magazine writers and newspaper reporters would show up tomorrow when they could take pictures of the games and entertainment and of Ledgeport itself with its houses dug into the rocky slope.

Merkka and Lucy ate and ate. They tried hanging out where Jay and his friends were; it was almost like being at a high school party.

Then the tables were cleared. Paper cloths, ripped from their taped corners and caught by the wind, flapped into the night. There was a brief flurry of excitement when some of the tattered paper snagged on a branch and burst into flame, but it went out all by itself. And in the quiet moment that followed, everyone was called to gather around the tables for the awards.

There was a lot of jostling and crowding. Lucy caught sight of her parents and went one way; Merkka remained where she could be sure of seeing the table with the important townspeople. She was thinking that if she won money for her cheer, she might try to buy back some of the sheep she had traded to Ben. Ben! It would be awful if he didn't win something too. But at least he had the pleasure of seeing his weapons carrier picture on the wall inside Gramary's buses.

Russell Leeward made a speech about how Ledgeport was great and so was its future. He introduced the judge, who was great too.

That reminded Merkka that she had to get back the things he had borrowed. She was glad Gramary had stayed away from this celebration. Craning to see everyone at the table, Merkka was startled to discover Mrs. Cope seated beside the judge. What was she doing here? Merkka had never really believed that she would come.

The awards began with the youngest kids, and Ben received third prize for his drawing of a bell buoy and a flying fish. Dad carried him through the crowd on his shoulders. Merkka couldn't see what was handed up to him, but Nancy Jenkins held up her second prize, one of those model sailboats the tourists buy at the Variety Store. Merkka hoped Ben would be satisfied with that. She hoped he didn't wish she had left his weapons carrier entered.

The awards went on. When Lucy won first prize in her age group, Mr. Leeward announced that her model would stay in the Town Hall on a special shelf. As people made room for her to leave with her prize, Merkka shouted to get her attention. Lucy squeezed through, waving a book. Merkka guessed that someone must have asked Lucy's parents what she would like. Merkka wondered what Mom and Dad suggested for her. In just a moment she would find out.

Only the next award was in the fourteen-to-eighteen-year-old group. They had forgotten to call Merkka's name.

Lucy paused beside her and whispered, "Why didn't you tell me your mother's pregnant?"

"What?" Merkka stared at her in amazement.

"I'm your best friend. You should've told me she's going to have a baby."

"Wait a minute," Merkka said. She couldn't digest this, not now when they had passed right by her name without calling it.

She tried to find an answer, but no words came. Awards were being handed out to grown-ups now. Nothing made any sense.

"Listen," said Lucy, turning her attention to the announcement of the grand prize. But there was some confusion at the table. Russell Leeward and Harley Sprague were speaking together. Then they turned to the judge. Straining, still listening for her own name, Merkka heard, " . . . wasn't submitted." And then the judge spoke so quietly Merkka couldn't hear him. And then "It was? By Mrs. Cope? Are you sure? Well . . . well . . ." Mrs. Cope said something else. After that Mr. Leeward informed the town of Ledgeport that Mary Weir had won the grand prize for a sculpture. A sculpture that happened to be lashed to the wreck in the outer harbor.

"Isn't that wonderful?" Lucy shouted through the cheering and clapping. "I'm really sorry you didn't win something too," she added. "At least you have something terrific to look forward to. A baby."

Merkka turned and ran into the throng. She ran like a sheep that is separated from its flock, without any sense of direction, in utter panic. Somehow people made room for her before she could hurt them or herself.

As soon as she broke away from the green, she headed downhill. Into the house and out again and down the steps to Gramary. She could hear herself yelling as she charged into the buses, where Gramary and Charlie were at work and belting out, "Shall We Gather at the River." Charlie was pumping a ratchet hoist while Gramary tightened a cable across from him. Merkka stood there, her heart pounding, her ears throbbing. "The bee-yew-ti-ful river," they sang.

"It's not fair," she screamed at them. "Not fair. Everyone knew but me. Everyone. Lucy got a book. I get a baby."

Gramary climbed down from the ladder. "Hush," she said.

"And you won!" Merkka shouted at her. "You'll be rich and famous!"

They could hear voices all around the buses. Jet barked and barked. "Mary Weird!" someone called from outside. "Trick or Treat!"

Charlie went to the door to ask them what they wanted. Several voices informed him they had come for the watch dog. Not this one out here, they explained, as Jet, still barking, backed up the steps and into the bus. They had come for the watch dog on the wreck.

Gramary joined Charlie in the doorway. She told the people outside she had given Suzy Cope the watchdog, and they told her that Mrs. Cope wanted it brought ashore. Gramary advised them to sober up and wait for daylight before going out to the wreck, but they insisted on fetching back the grand prize at once. "Hey!" one of them told her. "This is your big night, you know. Halloween!"

"Well, take flashlights," she said through their laughter. "And a knife to cut away the pot warp. And don't go falling overboard."

That made them laugh some more. Stumbling into things and each other, they surged around and onto Water Street.

By the time Mom and Dad and Ben showed up at home, half the town had drifted down to the waterfront. Several boats were launched, two of them fouled in mooring lines.

In all the commotion, Merkka slipped away to her room. Maybe if she kept to herself no one would notice how stupid she'd been. Standing there on the green waiting for her name to be called, certain she'd been overlooked. And she must be the only person in Ledgeport dumb enough to have missed what everyone else already knew about Mom, even though it was her own mother who had been sick for so long and different-acting. Probably Darleen had guessed weeks and weeks ago.

Ben soon came up after her. "Did you see what I won?" he exclaimed, without waiting for an answer. "I wonder if they'll give Gramary a boat. Maybe a truck."

Merkka had the lobster-feeling in her hands. It felt like something hard and squirming with terrible pincers going at her. She had to hurl it away from her. "Mom's going to have a baby." There. She had thrown it with all her might at Ben.

But he didn't seem to hear or feel it. He told her Mr. Leeward was mad because those guys out on the wreck were drunk and if they drowned he'd be blamed.

"Mom's going to have a baby!"

"No, she's not. And if anyone gets drowned, then the harbor-master—"

"She is. A baby."

"She can't, Merkka. There's no room for a baby."

"She's going to anyway."

Ben looked across the space between their beds. "Where will she put it?"

Merkka shrugged. The lobster came scuttling back into her arms.

Ben went to the door. "Mom!" he shouted. "Mom, are we really going to have a baby?"

Mom came first, Dad right behind her.

"Who told you?"

"Merkka."

Mom and Dad looked at Merkka.

"Everyone knows. Everyone knew but me."

"We waited to be sure everything was all right."

"Where will it sleep?" asked Ben.

"With us, for a while," Mom answered.

"Then here," Merkka told him meanly. "Where you keep your trucks."

He turned from her to Mom and Dad. "Do I have to move my things?"

"Maybe we'll work something else out," Mom offered.

Dad walked over to Merkka. "Mom wasn't feeling well. We didn't want you to worry."

Merkka could feel those lobster claws bite right through to her bones. "When will it be born?" she asked.

Mom said, "In the spring. End of March."

"Oh, boy!" said Ben. "When's March?"

"After Christmas," Dad told him with a smile. "After the snow and the winter storms. With the first flowers maybe."

Sure, flowers, thought Merkka. The only things that would bloom around this house were made of steel and iron.

Long after Ben fell asleep she lay staring into darkness. Gradually the last of the shouts in the harbor and the town subsided. Trick or treat, nothing had turned out the way it should. "I hope it rains," she whispered like a witch casting a spell. She imagined the pumpkins all over town sputtering in candle wax and fog and blinking briefly, one by one, before going out.

CHAPTER 23:

Which Witch

Of course I knew those guys were just kidding around when they told Gramary that Halloween was her night. But I couldn't help feeling they were just a bit leery of her. Spooked.

I wouldn't want people to feel that way about me.

But when I woke up on Saturday morning and saw that Ledgeport Appreciation Day was a washout, I knew it was my fault. I was the only person in the whole town who could have wished for rain. I had done it out of spite. I was the witch.

Most of the events had to be canceled. The rest were moved to the school auditorium, which wasn't big enough for everyone, especially everyone in dripping foul-weather gear.

Mrs. Cope had to talk Gramary into putting in an appearance. Gramary said she didn't have time, but when Mrs. Cope said she planned to offer the watch dog up for auction, with the proceeds going to help people who lost their jobs at the fish plant, Gramary agreed to go and receive her prize, which was money. Which would also go into a fund for those who were out of work.

The judge, who drove Mrs. Cope from the inn to the Weirs' house and brought with him Gramary's things, offered to buy some and to put others on exhibition in his gallery. He picked up on Mrs. Cope's plan to auction the watch dog. Ledgeport, he pointed out, could hold a really big auction later on to benefit all those who lost out on selling things because of the rain.

Gramary went upstairs to put on the dress she wore to meetings of the Ladies' Missionary Society. Mrs. Cope and the judge waited for her in the living room. Looking out of the window, the judge caught sight of the pinwheel disks down in the yard and asked about them. Mrs. Cope turned to Merkka, who had stood in the background without uttering a word.

"They're part of Mr. Brackett's hay rake," she said.

"Mary should call them 'The Sunne in Splendour,'" Mrs. Cope declared.

"She's working on them," Merkka supplied. "They're not finished."

The judge turned to Merkka with a smile. "There's plenty of time," he told her. "You can help by keeping track of everything your Gramary does. Don't let anyone take anything away."

Merkka wanted to point out that the disks belonged to Mr. Brackett, who could take them away whenever he liked, but when she opened her mouth to speak, she heard herself saying, "Wasn't my cheer fitting for the contest?"

"Your cheer?" The judge gave her question some thought. Then he said, "I think the problem goes the other way. It's too fitting."

She didn't know what he meant by that, but she was afraid to say so. She was afraid she might burst into tears.

The judge gave her a long look before he spoke again. "I

hope you write some more. I hope you write about what's fitting for yourself."

With relief, Merkka heard Gramary clumping down the stairs. In another moment the judge would be gone; she would never have to see him again.

"I'm quite sure," he told her softly, "that the magic words are in you."

"I know," she blurted, thinking of the rain she had made out of spite. "But they can make a lot of trouble too."

Mrs. Cope, overhearing, said, "Anything worthwhile is trouble. Don't you forget that, Mary Weir."

Gramary remarked as she joined them, "Trouble is my middle name, and there's one or two people here in town who aren't likely to forget it."

"I was speaking to *this* Mary Weir," Mrs. Cope informed Gramary. "Nobody needs to boost *your* confidence." She invited Merkka to ride up to the school with them. Merkka, who had decided to stay home, couldn't refuse without showing what a poor sport she was.

At the school she sat through speeches and a band concert. She clapped along with everyone else when Mr. Leeward announced that Gramary's prize money was going to the town and that later on there would be a big auction in Ledgeport with antiques and crafts and art to raise even more money to help people who were out of work and needed to buy food and gas and that.

Lucy, waving to Merkka, started up the aisle. Other kids were walking out, too, and drifting over to the gym. Merkka joined them. There was cider and Halloween cookies to make up for the sodden fish. But after fooling around awhile, Merkka decided to take her gloomy mood back home. She wanted to be alone, and she was sure she could count on the rest of the family staying on for what remained of Ledgeport Appreciation Day.

She had the house to herself and Jet for company, but she

could hear that Gramary was already back and at work with Charlie in the buses. They were singing, "I found my thril-l-l, on Blueberry Hill, on Blueberry Hill when I found you . . ." No amount of rain could drown out those voices.

Poor baby, Merkka thought. Poor unsuspecting baby to be born into this family.

A knock on the door made her jump. Most people walked in as they knocked. Jet started to bark.

When Merkka opened the door, there was a squat figure under a poncho, who said, "Mary Weir?"

"Yes," Merkka answered. She peered at the face as the poncho hood was pushed back. Maybe the stranger was a reporter from a big city newspaper.

He looked at her doubtfully. "I'm looking for Mary Weir."

"Oh," she said, "you mean my grandmother. She's working. Out."

"I think she'd like to talk to me," he said. "I'm a dealer."

"You can tell me whatever it is," Merkka told him, "and I'll see she gets the message."

"Big money," he declared, handing Merkka a little white card with his name and telephone number on it. "Big money if she doesn't talk to anyone but me. Got it?"

Merkka stared at his chubby fingers and his smooth pink cheeks. He had the look of a grown-up baby, a giant baby person. "I'll tell her," Merkka replied.

It was time for him to go, but he stepped toward the living room, his eyes on the seat from the Hudson car. Then he looked up and caught sight of Gramary's old mirror with the picture on the top. "What's this?" He lifted it off the nail and examined it closely.

Merkka said it was her grandmother's mirror. She felt she had to explain about it being so splotchy, so she told the man that no one minded that you couldn't see in it very well because they had a better mirror in the bathroom.

"Maybe your granny would like to sell this one," he remarked.

"You can ask her when you see her."

"Or you could surprise her, sell the old mirror, and get a brand-new one to hang there on the wall."

Merkka shook her head.

"Hey," he said, "you might make a little money for yourself on the side."

"How much?" she asked. "How much would a new one cost?"

He shrugged. "Ten, maybe fifteen. I might give you twenty for this old one."

Merkka thought about that. Maybe there was still some way to keep this weekend from being a dead loss. "What if a new one costs more?"

"Twenty-five," he said. He started for the door.

Voices from the buses swelled with a fresh hymn, "Rocked in the Cradle of the Deep." The singing rose and was dashed by the rain racket before it could fill the room.

"Who's singing?" asked the dealer.

"Charlie Budge. I mean," Merkka added quickly, "he's probably got the radio on."

The dealer hefted the mirror. "How's about my offer?"

"Thirty," she told him.

"You drive a hard bargain," he said. Without letting the mirror go, he reached into his pocket, pulled out a wad of bills, and counted out three tens. "Anything else to sell?"

Merkka shook her head. Suddenly she felt uneasy. The man had been too eager to pay what she had asked. She said, reaching out, "Let me see it a minute."

But the dealer held on as he backed toward the door.

Now Merkka was sure she had done something wrong. For a moment they struggled, she to wrest the mirror from him, he to keep it out of her reach. Then Jet moved between them, forcing them apart. He was growling too. Merkka had never heard him growl before. Afraid for Jet, she grabbed his collar. The dealer wasted no time getting away.

When Mom and Dad and Ben came home, they had the floor

tiles Mom had bought at the bargain corner. There was one full box and one with leftovers, maybe enough for the kitchen floor.

Merkka asked if that meant they would never move. Mom told her it would make the house nicer while they were there and easier to sell later on. So Merkka examined the tiles with interest. They had a pattern of tan and yellow crosses on what looked like pebbles. Maybe Merkka would be able to find a mirror to match. Maybe she was all right after all.

By the middle of the afternoon the rain let up. A dim watery light filtered through the clouds. The harbor glistened.

Gramary and Charlie sang, "You sure been good to me. Oh, it's Lord! Lord! Lord! You sure been good to me, 'cause you've done what the world couldn't do!"

"I can't stand it," Mom told Dad. "Just listen to them. Everyone's going to hate us because of her mess. You've got to stop her."

Dad said, "All right. I'll talk to her after I take Mrs. Cope out to the island. But I think you're making too much of what Russ and Ruth tell you."

"Sam! The only people you ever talk to are your wharf friends. They're all on her side. But now that she's won that grand prize, you think Russell's going to let her get away with what she's doing?"

"I don't know," Dad responded. "Honestly, I don't even know what to object to." He went out, leaving Mom with her tiles and the kitchen floor.

Mom made Merkka and Ben help her clear everything out of the kitchen. When Gramary came in to use the bathroom, there was so much confusion there was no danger of her missing her mirror.

"Start at the center," Gramary advised as she made her way across the kitchen to the side door.

"Why?" asked Mom, who was testing the sticky stuff on the back of a tile. All you had to do was peel away some paper and press the tile down where you wanted it to stay.

"Because if your tiles don't come out even, you don't have to cut ones to fit where they show the most."

"Oh." Mom fussed and fiddled awhile. Then she said, "There is no center. Not on this floor." But Gramary wasn't there to hear her. She was back at work in the buses with Charlie, who was starting up another song. "That old black magic's got me in its spell . . . ," he sang.

Merkka decided to go over to Lucy's house. Ben went out to the yard. When Merkka came home just after dark, she found tiles in rows beginning in front of the sink. They didn't reach all the way to the side door or even to the middle of the floor. Mom was in the living room on Gramary's sofa with her feet up. Dad was standing there telling her it's best to start tiles at the center.

"Don't," Mom groaned. "I'm no good at this."

Gramary and Ben came into the kitchen from the outside steps, and Ben shouted, "Look what Mom did!"

Gramary paused in the doorway to the living room. "We can finish the floor after supper," she told Mom.

"Supper," declared Mom in a leaden voice. "There isn't any."

"We'll have grilled cheese," said Gramary. "I'll do it."

"I don't know how you have so much energy." Mom sounded as though she didn't approve of energy.

"When I was carrying Sam," Gramary replied, "I was always looking for some place to put my feet up."

"Why didn't you just put him down?" asked Ben.

"Come on," Dad said. "We'll help Gramary get supper and let Mom rest."

But after supper Mom didn't want to get out the tiles again, so Gramary went back to work in the buses. Before long Charlie joined her. And Mom, sending Merkka and Ben to bed because it had been such an exciting weekend, reminded Dad that he had promised to talk to his mother. "Think what it's going to be like with the baby," Merkka could hear Mom urging. "We might still get the Haskell Gray house if you'd only try."

Ben sat with Merkka on the upstairs landing, but when nothing more was said, he got bored and went to bed. Merkka, using Jet as a cushion, settled down to listen.

When Dad went out to get Gramary, she brought Charlie in with her. Merkka could hear someone clattering the kettle on the stove.

"What's up, Sam?" Gramary asked. "Something bothering you?"

Dad seemed to have trouble beginning. Finally Mom stepped in. "It's the buses, Mary. The buses, and everyone worrying about what's happening down here."

"Well, they won't have to worry much longer," Gramary answered. "I might as well tell you, ease your minds. I have to finish this thing here, but I'm moving right along with Charlie to help. And when we're done, you can do what you like with it. All of it."

"Really?" That was Mom.

"It'll be up to you and Sam. You can hold on or sell, or some of each."

"But it's yours, Ma," Dad said to her. "We didn't mean we wanted—"

"I'll be moving out," Gramary told him.

"Moving by yourself?" Mom exclaimed. "Oh, no, Mary!"

"Yes. It's what I've decided to do. What we've decided. Charlie and me."

Mom and Dad were talking at the same time. Merkka scootched down three steps, but all she could see was Mom's back in the doorway between the living room and the kitchen. She couldn't see the others at all.

"We don't want anyone to know yet," Gramary went on. "Otherwise young Dogfish Leeward will think it was his doing. We don't want to give him the satisfaction."

Dogfish! Merkka slid down another step, then had to grab Jet, who thought she was on her way downstairs. In the last few days Gramary had thrown away a couple of models of dogfish. "Not sharklike enough," she'd explained to Ben. "It wants to look mean." Now Gramary was saying Dogfish instead of Russell. What was she up to?

"We're getting married," Gramary declared. "Me and Charlie."

Merkka clutched at Jet.

"We didn't even want to tell you. We didn't want arguments, not from anyone."

"How long—" Dad started to ask her.

"We decided out on the island. Now you can get used to the idea. But we'd appreciate you keeping it to yourselves." Gramary began to laugh. "Bev looks like she swallowed a sea urchin."

"No, no I—" Mom was stammering. "I never thought—"

"Nor did I." This was Charlie speaking up finally. "I waited so long I nearly forgot what I was waiting for."

"Well," said Dad. "Well." He seemed to have as much trouble ending this conversation as beginning it.

The water kettle rattled on the stove and someone took it off. Merkka crept back up to bed. For a while she listened to the jumble of voices downstairs without trying to catch what was said. All she could think of was that night when Charlie Budge had thrown Jet into the water and sped away from him. Gramary would never marry him if she knew that. But what if she didn't believe Merkka? What if she went ahead and made a fool of herself anyhow? What would happen to Jet?

When Merkka heard Dad getting up in the morning, she waited until he left for the boat before padding downstairs to Gramary.

"Are you awake?" she whispered.

Gramary's voice came full and deep. "Yes."

"I heard last night. About you and Charlie."

"Oh." There was a long pause. "I'd be obliged if you said nothing just yet."

"Can I tell Lucy?"

Gramary switched on the lamp. She was sitting up, her hair flat against the side of her head as though from a wind coming at her. But there was no wind, only sleepy warmth.

"Are you going away to make room for the baby?"

"I'm going away to make room for myself," said Gramary.

"What will Ben do without you?" Even as she asked this, Merkka imagined them like other families. They could fix up the living room and plant flowers in the back.

"He'll spend as much time with me as he likes. And next year he'll be in first grade. He'll be on to other things."

"I could never get used to you marrying Charlie Budge," Merkka declared. "Never." Then she added. "Couldn't you just try it out for a while without getting married?"

Gramary smiled. "I've thought of it. We've both thought of it. I think your mom and dad would feel better if we make it legal."

"But you'll miss us," Merkka pressed.

"I'll miss you and I won't miss you. There's not much to moving out to Limeburner Point. I won't be taking any furniture and that."

Merkka stared at the place on the wall where the mirror had hung. The time had come to break the news to Gramary about it. "Wait a minute," Merkka whispered. She scudded upstairs to get the three ten-dollar bills. She brought them to Gramary and told her about the dealer. "And there's big money," she concluded, "if you don't talk to anyone but him about your things."

"Too late," Gramary said. "But I'll take the card. I'll have a word with him by and by."

"Are you mad at me?" Merkka asked her.

"I'm mad at him, not you. But you shouldn't do things like that. The mirror belonged to my father's mother. It was in the family a long time."

Merkka said, "Everything I did this weekend was bad."

Gramary looked surprised. "Real bad?"

Merkka nodded.

"How bad?" Gramary coaxed.

"I made it rain. I spoiled Ledgeport Appreciation Day."

Gramary laughed out loud. Then she drew Merkka against her in a massive hug. "Don't worry," she said, still laughing. "So did I."

CHAPTER 24:

Beyond the Bounds

*Almost overnight Gramary became a celebrity. Not the
way she was already known in town, but with people
from away that had never even heard of Ledgeport
before. One newspaper in Boston had a whole page
about her. People called her on the telephone, but she
never spoke to them. And the more she ignored those
people, the harder they tried to get her.*

*Charlie liked talking to them. Where his sister lived in
Massachusetts there were lots of arts and crafts. It
didn't take long to pick up what tickled the buyers'
fancy. But no one else knew how to talk to those people.*

*Before Mrs. Cope went to Florida for the winter, she
made everyone promise to hold onto Gramary's things.
She also insisted that they schedule the big Ledgeport
auction for when she could be there. That would give
them plenty of time to collect items to sell.*

*Russell Leeward talked about the coming auction
whenever he had the chance. He told every newspaper
and magazine writer how proud he was of Ledgeport's
Mary Weir. He was also proud that his campaign to
bring out local talent had led to the discovery of this
outstanding artist.*

"'Outstanding,'" Ed Ingalls read aloud when Blanche brought the newspaper with his lunch. It was noon on Saturday. Merkka and Ben were in the boat shed picking up some things for Gramary. "Can you hear Russ saying that? 'Outstanding'?"

Blanche dished out macaroni and cheese. "You're awfully hard on Russell. At least he's trying to change his tune now. Spike, will you have some macaroni? There's plenty here."

Spike stood up to receive his plateful, and Merkka asked Ed if she could take the broken bilge pump.

"If Mary can't fix it again, she might as well have it." Ed pulled the plunger free, then handed the parts back to Merkka.

"At least the pressure's off Mary," Blanche pointed out.

Ed shook his head. "Don't be too sure. You know Mary calls him Dogfish. You want to watch out how you handle one of them little sharks."

No sooner had Blanche left to go up to Stan's Market than Ed thrust his plate at Merkka, got up, and went over to the salt cod hanging in the doorway. Peeling off a strip of the cod, he returned to his chair to eat it.

Merkka shared the delicious lunch with Ben and had the plate safely returned to Ed's lap before Blanche returned to clean up.

"Very tasty," Ed told her, scraping the plate in her presence. He always said that; she always looked pleased.

When Ben and Merkka got home, Gramary wouldn't let them, or even Jet, stay in the yard. She and Charlie were going to pop the rest of the roof out, and it was tricky work. If the hoist let go or a cable broke, it could go shooting off in any direction.

Merkka watched from the living room window. Charlie, on a ladder, lashed the hoist hook to ring bolts protruding from the roof. The other end of the cable was attached to the A-frame. Gramary removed the crossbeams she'd jammed in when she removed the roof supports. All of it looked tricky, especially when Charlie slipped and landed on his hands and knees. He stopped himself from falling by grabbing the cable. Gramary yelled up to him. Slowly he clambered to his feet again and with great care hauled himself onto the A-frame and began to pump the handle of the hoist.

Merkka thought, If Charlie falls and hurts himself, Gramary won't marry him. But she was afraid to wish that it would happen. Her thought went on its dangerous track. Gramary had spent years caring for her invalid husband. Nothing would make her do that again, especially at her age.

Ben and Jet pressed in beside Merkka. Gramary watched from below. At first Charlie pumped rapidly. Then he slowed. Easy, Gramary seemed to be warning him. He raised the handle, lowered it, raised it once more. There was a report like a thunderclap. Jet ducked back and scrambled up the stairs. An entire section of the bus roof had blown out. Charlie froze, still gripping the hoist handle. Then Gramary threw up her arms. Charlie stood up straight and reversed the ratchet until he could unhitch the hoist and let it slowly down.

It was safe now. Ben turned and dashed out the side door and down the steps. Jet peered down from the landing, then retreated once more.

"Charlie, row your boat ashore . . . ," Gramary started to sing at the top of her lungs. "Hallelujah!"

Merkka, still at the window, caught her breath in amazement. At last she could see what Gramary had been up to with the buses. They were joined, with the roof rising to a peak along the center line where they had been separate before. The peak looked just like the keel of a boat, a huge upturned boat with a snubbed bow. Merkka knew that the transformation had been under way for weeks. Only now, like magic, all was revealed. The buses were no more; in their place, like a stranded whale, this boat-shaped hulk loomed on the foreshore.

Merkka tried to coax Jet down to the door, but he only turned tail and made for her room. Figuring he would dig himself a nest in her bed and stay there for the rest of the day, she walked out of the house alone and up Landing Road to School Street. But no one was home at the Starobins except Jay, and he was doing homework. Merkka caught a glimpse of a dictionary beside his report. Just in case this dictionary was different from her school one, she asked him if she could look up Gramary. But he didn't want her disturbing his things, so he looked it up for her. He pointed to a word, in tiny print, which she had to bend over to read: "Gramarye," with one m and an extra e after the y. "Occult learning," the dictionary told her; "magic." She was so astonished that she grabbed at the dictionary and nearly messed up the paper Jay was writing on. She was sorry. She just wanted to look up *occult*.

Jay groaned, but he turned to the O's to find occult. "No," he warned, waving her off, "I'll read it. 'Occult. Beyond the bounds of ordinary knowledge. Mysterious, secret.' Okay?"

Merkka could scarcely believe her ears. "Now go back to what it says about Gramarye," she told him.

"No, you just saw it. I'm busy."

"But what exactly does it mean?" she pressed.

"How should I know? What it says, is all."

Merkka couldn't bear it. What was the good of a dictionary that gave you explanations you couldn't understand? She asked Jay when his father would be home, but he had no idea. He had the house to himself for a change. He had work to do.

Thanking him, puzzling over what she had just learned, Merkka let herself out the porch way. A fresh, sharp wind had sprung up, hurling leaves and branches every which way. As she started down Landing Road, Mr. Leeward and a strange man passed her and turned onto Gray Street.

"Hello there," Mr. Leeward said to Merkka. Then he stopped and informed the stranger that Merkka was Mary Weir's grandaughter.

Something made Merkka say, "You're going to the Haskell Gray house."

"Smart," Mr. Leeward remarked to the stranger.

"You're selling the Haskell Gray house," she said hopelessly.

"How did you guess that?" the stranger wanted to know.

"I didn't guess," Merkka replied. "I just knew. I knew," she went on, "beyond the bounds of ordinary knowledge." Only it didn't help knowing. What she needed to be able to do was assure Mr. Leeward that if he could only wait a little longer, Mom and Dad would buy the house.

"Well," said the stranger, "that's quite a mouthful."

Merkka, her heart sinking, realized that Mr. Leeward would see the busboat long before he learned that Gramary was leaving the waterfront. He would see the busboat the way Mr. Sprague had seen the shirt, a sign that Gramary would not give up. There was no way to hold onto the Haskell Gray house now.

Going down Landing Road, Merkka experimented with leaning into the wind. She found that she could tilt farther than the street did. It took a strong wind to hold you up like that. Gramary would be able to tell just how strong it was.

Letting the wind hold her, Merkka slanted down the slanting hill. When she started to fall, she righted herself, spread her arms, and thought about billowing sails. Next she thought about flying, until it reminded her of broomsticks. Then she tried to think about something else. She told herself that if she believed in witches, she might think Gramary had held back the wind until the busboat roof was safely popped. The wind, free now from any spell, carried her magically, though not exactly smoothly, to her own door.

Ben was coming through from the outside steps at the same time Merkka came in from Water Street.

"Gramary's crying," he said, holding onto the door. "She was working on the dogfish. I think she hurt her eye."

"Isn't Charlie there?" asked Merkka.

Ben shook his head. "Gramary does the dogfish all by herself."

Merkka knew that. Gramary had been making a dogfish figurehead while working on the buses. There had been many models before she settled on the dogfish of her choice. Merkka had wondered who would want such an ugly figurehead, and such a big one, on the prow of a boat. Someone from away, she had supposed; someone with one of those old-fashioned schooners. Only now did it come to her that Gramary intended the dogfish for her own busboat. Just wait till Harley Sprague and Russell Leeward saw it there.

Merkka let go of the door, which slammed shut. The whole house shook. Merkka was shaking, too, shaking with anger because Gramary had ruined their chances for the Haskell Gray house. "Where's Mom?" she asked. Mom could take care of Gramary's hurt eye.

"Somewhere," Ben said. "With Mrs. Leeward, I think."

They had to hang onto the rail as they made their way down the steps. It was easy to hurt your eye today, Merkka thought. Everything small and loose was swirling around in circles. The inner harbor frothed with spume. Lines and wharf gear whipped overhead and clanked against rigging.

Gramary was seated on the bottom step of the busboat, her legs spread wide, her hands clutching her face.

"Gramary?" Ben approached timidly. He started to cry.

"Shut up," Merkka snapped at him.

"S'all right," Gramary said through her hands. The words came thick and muffled.

Merkka tried to draw the hands away and found them surprisingly yielding. Staring into Gramary's face, it was hard to tell whether she was actually crying or just recovering from some kind of blow. The weeping eye kept twitching, and something wasn't right about Gramary's cheek. All the way down to her mouth.

"What happened?" asked Merkka.

Gramary tried to look at her, but her eye wouldn't stay still. "Moment," Gramary got out. "Time."

"Can you come inside? I don't think you should be in this wind." Merkka was certain that something had blown into Gramary's eye.

But Gramary didn't seem to know how to step up into the busboat. With Merkka's help, she turned around. She held on to the side of the door. She could go no farther.

Merkka turned back to Ben. "Go and get someone," she told him.

"Who?"

"Go to Ed's. Go to Stan's Market. Anywhere. Anyone we know." Then she eased Gramary around and helped her sink back onto the step.

Gramary's hands went back to her face. "Blowing up a storm," she mumbled.

Merkka tried to shield her from the bits of swirling things, from the wind itself. She stood with her back to the outdoors, but she couldn't block the gusts. "Can you see?" she asked Gramary.

Gramary nodded. "Jus' res'," she said. "S'all right." She slumped forward over her ample lap.

By the time Ed and Spike came running to them, Gramary was holding up her head and trying to wipe off her face and chin. Their concern gave way to relief when she batted at their hands and told them to quit bugging her. But even after they had helped her around the long way to Water Street and into the house, no one could get a clear idea of what had happened.

"A spell" was all she could tell them from the sofa. "A turn. Nothing really." She wouldn't hear of going to the doctor or calling Sam on the *Little Mary*. "I'll nap," she promised. "If you stop clucking over me." The words sounded like her, but the way she spoke wasn't normal. Her mouth wouldn't close on the right side. She kept dabbing at it to wipe off saliva that dribbled from it. "Go on," she insisted. "Take Ben." She pulled the lid down over her jumpy eye.

Spike led Ben out of the living room. Ed said, "That's right, Mary. When you wake up you'll be right as rain." But he looked worried, and he could hardly tear himself away.

"Stay," Gramary said to Merkka. "Stay, my darling."

Merkka had never heard her say darling before. Except for the song she sometimes sang that went, "Charlie is my darling!" Merkka asked, "Do you want me to get Charlie?"

"Charlie," Gramary repeated. "Not now."

"I could make you some tea," Merkka offered.

"That's it," Gramary responded. "I'll have a little chickadee."

Merkka hesitated. Then she went into the kitchen and turned the stove on under the kettle and put a teabag in a mug. Mom came in before the water boiled, saw Gramary lying on the sofa, and said, "Oh, I was just going to lie down myself. I'll go upstairs."

"Gramary hurt her eye," Merkka told Mom. She poured the water, set down the kettle, and burst into tears.

Mom whipped around. "Her eye?"

"No," whispered Merkka. Because all of a sudden she knew it wasn't that at all. It was something else mysterious and terrible that had come inside of Gramary like the tide after a storm. Whatever it was that had seized Gramary was beyond the bounds of ordinary knowledge, and still beyond that, beyond Gramary's power.

Mom tiptoed over to the sofa. A moment later she came back into the kitchen. She put her arms around Merkka and told her that it was all right, Gramary was just fine now, but not to bother her with the tea because she was fast asleep.

CHAPTER 25:

Coming to Terms

When Mom put her arms around me, I could feel the baby inside her. We were holding each other. And when we did that, we held the baby too.

By morning Gramary was much better, although her eye and mouth still drooped a little, and once in a while she said something that didn't seem to say what she meant. Dad insisted on taking her to the hospital. They were gone all day. And when she came home, Gramary was worn out from all the tests they'd given her.

Merkka imagined pages and pages of true-false questions even though she really had some idea about hospital tests from watching television. "Were the tests hard?" she asked Gramary.

"Not bad." Gramary flexed her right hand. She stretched her fingers out with her left hand and kneaded them. "They've gone too deep," she said. "Fingers," she explained.

"To sleep," Merkka interpreted.

"Yes," said Gramary.

When the doctor called and wanted her back at the hospital again, she said she didn't have time for any more nonsense. But Charlie told her she'd better go so that they would know what they were in for.

The next afternoon when Merkka got home from school Gramary and Charlie were gone. They finally showed up singing at the top of their lungs. They brought a bakery cake with wedding bells on top and an enormous pizza that had bounced so hard in the back of Charlie's truck that all the pepperoni was stuck to the top of the cardboard box.

They reported that Gramary's spell had been a mild stroke. From now on she would have to take pills and watch what she ate.

"Is pizza all right?" asked Dad doubtfully.

Gramary said it was the last pizza of her life, and the same for the cake. Mom insisted that they would be given a proper party when they were married, including a wedding cake. Gramary reminded her that they didn't want anyone to know yet. The busboat still needed a few finishing touches.

"Must you?" pleaded Mom. "Can't you quit now?"

Gramary pulled and flexed the fingers of her right hand. "It's something I have to do," she said.

Mom got up and went into the living room and turned on the TV.

"She's some put out," Charlie said to Gramary. "Maybe you should reconsider."

"Bev's had a hard year," Dad reminded them.

Gramary sat in silence, her face sagging to the downturn of her mouth.

"Aren't we going to have pizza and cake?" Ben wanted to know.

"Cripes, yes," Charlie told him. "You bet we are."

Dad got Mom to rejoin them, but she stayed moody. Merkka looked at everyone seated around the table. Why didn't she feel glad that Gramary would be gone soon? Her eyes came to rest on Charlie dishing out slabs of mutilated pizza. Gramary was going to marry him so that Mom and Dad could clear up this place or sell it. Gramary couldn't bring herself to do either, because that would look as though she were giving in. All she could do was get married and move to Limeburner Point.

Merkka imagined the announcement in the *Muskeag News:* "Mary Weird weds former hog farmer and caretaker of Grace Island."

Merkka couldn't bite through the cold, rubbery cheese. She just kept gobbling it in until her mouth was stuffed. It was like trying to eat Playdoh. She had to leave the table.

In the living room she removed the wad of cheese and called softly to Jet. But he was sticking close to Ben to clean up driblets and crumbs. She went back to the kitchen and stuck the cheese under the table. Jet swallowed it down in one gulp.

"What about cake?" asked Charlie. "Don't you want some?"

Not from Charlie she didn't. But if she turned it down, Gramary would think Merkka was mad like Mom. "All right," she mumbled, spreading her fingers for Jet to lick clean.

"All right what?" said Mom.

Merkka sighed. "Please," she added. "Or thank you." Either magic word would do.

"Blows out of joint," commented Gramary.

"What?" asked Dad and Mom and Charlie all together.

"Nose," Merkka told them, pleased that she was the only one who could figure out Gramary's words. "She means me," Merkka added quickly. Out of joint was right. Because now that Merkka was getting what she had wanted, it was turning out wrong.

Someone, she decided, would have to stop Gramary before it was too late. Someone who understood beyond the bounds of ordinary knowledge.

But as the days went by, Merkka couldn't think of a way. She saw Gramary recover enough to go back to work on the

busboat. Charlie brought in a length of track from an old manure hauler; Gramary fitted it onto the keel and welded it in
place. Then she built up the prow until it was ready for the
figurehead. Merkka had forgotten that the dogfish would have
to go on upside down to conform to the appearance of the over-
turned boat. It was almost startling that way, a realistic stroke
that confirmed the transformation from buses to boat.

Meanwhile dealers descended on Ledgeport like blackflies in
June. And like blackflies they stuck to their hosts and bled
their houses dry of every old and used item they could get hold
of. In every issue of the *Muskeag News* the Greeleys dutifully
reminded people about the upcoming auction. They assured
residents that all those items carried off in dealers' vans could
sell for much more at a well-advertised auction and would help
the folk of Ledgeport at the same time. But the dealers delivered a different message: By spring those items might be a
dime a dozen; you could get your money now, not in some
problematic future.

"What they're really after," Ruth Leeward told Mom over a
tunafish sandwich, "is Mary's stuff. They all hope to make a
killing on her."

"A killing?" Ben sucked in his breath.

"Not a real killing," she explained. "It's just that everyone
wants your Gramary's things."

Mom said, "And the funny thing is she still doesn't care
about the money. She only wants to get even, not rich."

"Even with who?" Ben pursued.

A look passed between the grown-ups. Ruth Leeward shook
her head.

Mom said to her, not to Ben, "Mary doesn't like to be
pushed. She likes to have her own way."

And Mrs. Leeward replied, "I wish she could understand
how Russell's come to appreciate her since, well, all this. You
wouldn't believe what he got from one of those dealers for

Mary's—well, it's a metal bird he got hold of. He did real good with it."

Merkka spoke up. "That was Darleen's birthday present."

"That's all right," Mrs. Leeward said, "because Darleen's dad bought her brand-new Christmas boots with some of that money. She's better off with them than with that metal thing."

Merkka didn't reply to that. So much had happened that she hardly understood how she felt anymore. A few months ago she would have agreed with Mrs. Leeward; a few months ago she was sure that Mr. Leeward was on her side. She supposed that nothing much had changed with them. The change was in Gramary and in Merkka.

She didn't dare ask Gramary when she would leave. Maybe if no one said anything to provoke her, she would take her time about the move. But Merkka couldn't help worrying, because the busboat was finally finished.

She decided to confront Charlie Budge herself. She would do it alone. Only that was hard, going to Limeburner Point without even Jet for company. She seldom went there these days. There was no need, for Charlie Budge had the sheep in the barn now, Grace had turned out to be a ram lamb; Gramary was afraid that some of the ewes were bred. But Grace was over at Mr. Brackett's farm waiting for Ben to be willing to let him go. Everyone hoped there wouldn't be too many lambs come spring.

It was nearly dark when Merkka set out, so she hurried. A car passed her; she shrank into the weeds at the side of the road. Then headlights came at her from the opposite direction. She didn't need to get off the road, but she stood still to let the truck go by. Only it didn't. It stopped. Charlie rolled down the window of its cab. "Going somewhere?"

Merkka nodded.

"Get in," he said.

She climbed up and sat beside him.

"Where to?"

"I was going to see you."

Whistling the "Black Magic" tune, he drove until he came to a barway to a field. He backed up to it. "Now," he said, "we can go to my house or go home, whichever you want."

"Could we just stay here a minute?"

"Sure." He shut off the lights and the engine. He started whistling again, softly this time, between his teeth.

"It's about Gramary. About you and Gramary. I don't think she'll change her mind."

"You're right." Then he added, "But I guess she cares what you think. You'd like her to change her mind?"

Merkka nodded.

"What?"

"Yes."

"Why?"

Merkka drew a breath. "I saw you that night. Coming back from Grace Island, before you went away. You didn't see us in the harbor. And I'm sure Gramary didn't see what you did."

"What did I do?" He sounded puzzled.

"You picked something up. It looked heavy." If only she could keep her voice from quavering. "You threw it overboard."

Charlie sat quite still. Merkka's mouth was dry and hot. When would he say something?

"Is that it?"

She nodded again.

"Merkka, speak up. I can't see you that well."

"Yes," she said, and then, "If Gramary knew, she wouldn't marry you."

"Not marry me?" Charlie seemed to be turning some thoughts over. "I doubt that."

"She'd never live with anyone that did a thing like that."

"Cripes, Merkka, I don't know as I'd go that far. You could tell her," he suggested, "and see what she thinks."

"I can't," Merkka retorted. "She wouldn't believe me.

Unless," she challenged, facing him in the dark, "unless you told her yourself."

"Well, I suppose I could do that."

Merkka knew better than to trust him. "Would you tell her when I'm there too?"

There was quite a long pause. When Charlie finally spoke, he didn't sound puzzled anymore. He sounded irritated. "What is this? What's going on?"

Quickly she said, "Please, if you do that, I'll give you a sheep."

He said, "I can't believe this."

She answered stoutly, "It means a lot to me."

"How much? Two sheep?"

"All right. Two sheep."

"Three?"

"I've already given three to Ben."

"How about the dog then? Two sheep and a dog."

"No! How can you say that?"

"Cripes, he's mine already, you know."

"Not anymore!" she shouted. "You don't deserve him!" Opening the door, she fell to the ground. The grass was drenched with frost and slippery. There was better footing on the road, though. She set off at a run. Charlie came after her. She could hear him wheeze as he pounded along the dirt surface. "Stay away from me," she screamed at him. "If you don't stay away, I'll tell."

"Tell what?" he demanded, anger making him shrill.

"I'll tell that you chased me." She turned to face him. "I'll tell that you threw Jet into the harbor."

"Liar!" he shouted at her. He walked up to her. "Do you know how mean you are? Mary took care of you. She took care of Ben. You think she wants to baby-sit again at her age? You think she needs that?"

Merkka could feel hot tears on her face. Her throat was too clogged to speak.

He said, his voice back to normal, "It's one thing to bargain with sheep. It's another thing to lie."

"I wasn't. I didn't."

A car whizzed toward them. Charlie pulled her to one side. "We'll go back to the truck now," he told her. "I'll take you home."

Once they were back inside the cab, he asked, "Will you always feel this way about me?"

She wiped her nose on her sleeve. "Yes."

"I'm sorry," he said, "but it won't stop me being happy."

So he had won. She had got nowhere. "Anyway," she said, "I wasn't lying."

"I never threw the dog away. I left him, yes. Only I didn't know it at the time. Started back when I saw he wasn't with me, but then it was too dark. And I figured he'd make out all right. I'd left the bag of dog food out there. He could've torn into it. I never thought he'd come to harm. Never imagined him ending up on the wreck like that."

"It was all he could get to."

"Don't you see what I'm saying? I figured he'd jumped out when we were leaving Grace Island. See, he knew I was annoyed with him. I'd paid good money for him, and he wouldn't do nothing for me. I kept telling him to get the sheep, and the more I told him, the worse he was. Then he drove that one lamb right out on the cliff. There I was yelling at him to get it, and him pushing it over the edge. 'Course now I know that was the wrong thing to say."

What was Charlie talking about? What did a lamb have to do with it?

"I couldn't leave it there, could I?" Charlie went on. "Couldn't leave it lying there with its neck broke. So I had to climb all the way down and then carry it back to the boat, and all the time telling that dog what I thought of it. And I had to lug rocks along so I could sink the lamb. Only I was so fussed I forgot to throw it overboard until we were coming into Ledgeport."

Merkka tried to keep up with what he was telling her, but he was saying things that didn't mesh with what she had seen. With what she had thought she had seen. She said carefully, "You threw a lamb overboard?"

"In a bag," he said. "With some rocks. A big lamb, nearly grown. And it was just after that I noticed the dog wasn't in the boat." Charlie heaved a sigh. "I know Mary wouldn't like what happened, especially me hollering at the dog. But I don't mind if she finds out. It won't make no difference. She already knows I'm an old fool."

Merkka leaned back. A torn place in the upholstery was like a fist between the shoulder blades forcing her to straighten. Only she felt limp. Or foolish, as Charlie would say. She had been so sure of what had happened. Even after she'd tried to tell on Charlie and made Mr. Brackett mad at her, it had never once occurred to her that she might be wrong.

Just before they pulled up at the house, Charlie said, "I still don't know what this is all about. But I want to tell you, Merkka, your Gramary and me, we're going to do all right."

Merkka thought back over the months of blame and how every day it had set her against Charlie. She struggled for words. "Cripes," she finally managed to say to him, "then you better be careful, you better not go slipping and sliding on old bus roofs anymore."

"I hear you," he agreed. "Only that's no bus now. That's the bottom of a boat." In the light from the kitchen window she saw him smile at her. "Local color for the folks up the hill."

Figuring that now he could probably see her, too, she nodded one more time.

CHAPTER 26:

Caretalker

All the really major events in my life seemed to come together at the same time. First was Gramary and Charlie getting married, although they did it by themselves so there would be no fuss. It turned out they had arranged for it the day they came home with the pizza and cake.

In the beginning Ben minded a whole lot. Then he got used to going out to Limeburner Point almost every day, except when a gale was blowing, or a blizzard. Jet would go along with him. I think Jet just decided he had two homes now. But when Gramary started to jumble things more and more in her talk, Ben felt strange with her. Even though she still went on welding and making things for a while, it got different between them.

It wasn't the same for me either. By the time everyone else found out about Gramary and Charlie, it wasn't too awful at school. People figured they might get their

names in the papers if they said something nice about
Gramary. And when writers and artists came to see
Gramary, I was able to help because I was good at
figuring out what she meant to say.

She never stumbled over names, though. "This is
Merkka," she would tell them. "Merkka is my
caretalker." Charlie thought she meant granddaughter,
but I think caretalker is a real word she made out of all
the ones she had in mind about me. About us.

Only when things got worse, when her fingers
wouldn't hold onto the torch or a hammer or pliers any
longer, and when she had more trouble getting people to
understand, she stopped trying. She only wanted to see
us or her friends from the wharf. And even when she
was having a good time, her laughter came out funny,
like someone sobbing. Charlie always laughed with her
when that happened. But sometimes he would suddenly
get up and go away by himself, and once I found him in
the kitchen wiping his eyes with his hand. He never let
Gramary see that he was grieving. He would sing while
he did things for her, hymns like "Rocked in the Cradle
of the Deep" and "Eternal Father Strong to Save." He
even did it Gramary-style, belting out, "O hear us when
we cry to Thee for those in peril on the sea."

But he stopped singing "That Old Black Magic." You
won't hear Charlie singing those words anymore. That's
partly why I've written this. Because Charlie can't sing
them, the magic words, and Gramary can't use them. So
I figure it's up to me—Gramary's caretalker.

And I've written all this for you because you missed
out on the trouble with Gramary. You can't ever know

what it was like, what she was like. I wish I could show you with pictures, but I'd probably end up with a person knitting socks in a rocking chair. Even if I put her on the porch at Limeburner Point, that wouldn't make it true. Maybe Ben will draw pictures of some of Gramary's things that are going away to museums and rich people's houses. He could show you the watchdog the way it looked on Halloween before Gramary scrubbed it with steel wool and oil to clean off the rust and gunk that covered it from the wreck. All I can do is try to tell you with the right words, even though it will be a while before you can understand them.

Because you are another one of the major events of the year, even though you're so tiny you still fit in the bureau drawer, and the biggest thing about you is your name.

At first I minded that Caroline is so much more beautiful than Merkka or Mary, but I'm over that now. Dad says you will have to grow into your name; I think I'm growing into mine.

What with you coming and the excitement of the auction, no one's done much planning about what we'll do with this place, although Mom is still thinking about selling fried clams and lobster rolls, and Lucy says she's going to be a waitress here until she's old enough to be a sea captain.

The auction was a major event for the whole town, not just for us. By the time it happened there were new rumors about a mussel farm coming in and using the fish plant for packing. Everyone was hopeful about new

jobs. But the auction was still the biggest thing that
ever happened in Ledgeport.

Most years Mrs. Cope returned to Grace Island when spring
was well along. But this year was different. She came in March
and stayed at the Harbor View Inn. That was good for Ida and
Cliff Billings, who didn't usually have guests so early in the
season. Mrs. Cope told Dad she wanted to spend some time
with Gramary, and she told Gramary she was in Ledgeport to
see that the auction went off without a hitch.

Every household in town turned itself inside out to find
items the dealers had missed. Many people from away also donated things to the auction, antiques and quilts and paintings
and half-models of old sailing ships. They also came to bid and
buy.

It was a spectacle for Ledgeport and most certainly made up
for the washout back in the fall. Mrs. Cope, who donated the
watchdog in the first place, ended up buying it back as a gift
to the town. She said she wanted it placed on the green at the
other end from the war memorial. As far as Charlie and Ed and
the others could figure, that put it about squarely in front of
the entrance to Russell Leeward's real estate office. Mrs. Cope
also said she hoped the sculpture would watch over those who
needed watching from now on. The whole audience stood up
to applaud.

Merkka was amazed at what people would pay for Gramary's
things. The old herring sign from the cannery went for a huge
amount of money because it was used.

When all of Gramary's sculptures had been sold and antiques were being auctioned, Merkka caught sight of Charlie
and Mrs. Cope conferring at the back of the auditorium. Then
Charlie beckoned to Dad and to Ed Ingalls and they all left.

A little while later, Merkka saw one of Bob Brackett's hay
rake disks rolled onto the auditorium stage. All by itself like
that it looked like a giant orange-and-yellow sunflower.

The auctioneer finished selling marine hardware from an old Tancook whaler, went to the back of the stage to talk to Charlie, and returned to the microphone with wonderful news. Here was another item from Mary Weir's workshop. His voice boomed with the importance of this announcement. "Who'll start bidding on this magnificent sun symbol?"

Merkka heard a murmur stir through the audience. One of the art people stood up and objected because they hadn't had a chance to examine the thing beforehand.

"That's right," the auctioneer agreed. "This splendid piece is a find, a late entry."

Glancing all around, Merkka finally spotted Charlie at the rear of the auditorium. She scrambled through the crowd to him. "You can't sell that," she whispered. "It's one of the disks Gramary was supposed to fix so that Bob Brackett could sell his pinwheel rake."

"No need to tell the world, Merkka. Bob'll get more money this way than he ever could with the thing repaired. Now show me the man that bought Mary's mirror."

"But Gramary didn't make that sun!" Merkka protested. "Anyway it's not a sun, it's a—"

Charlie clapped a hand over her mouth. "No one said Mary made it. Where's that man? Point him out to me."

By now the bidding was climbing furiously. Some Ledgeport people were beginning to chortle and whisper among themselves. Merkka pulled Charlie's hand away and whispered too. "It's wrong!"

"Look," Charlie countered, "none of your real art people are bidding. It's just them dealers. See that lady on the aisle? She's the one that paid a few dollars for Reggie's old decoys and sold them right off for thousands. And I expect Ed's working on the dealer that bought Blanche's grandpa's sextant and paid for it with a toaster oven. Doesn't matter which of them gets the sun, but I'd like to make sure the fellow that took Mary's mirror has a chance at it."

Merkka watched the people bidding and the people looking

on. There was no doubt that most of the town was enjoying the show immensely. And Mr. Leeward was so busy being interviewed that he was missing all of it.

Merkka cast her eyes over the audience. It wasn't hard to find the dealer with the baby face. She pointed to him, but she couldn't help asking Charlie, "Won't they think Gramary cheated them?"

Charlie didn't take time to answer her. He was pressing through to reach the dealer. Then he stood beside him, dropping a word now and then.

Merkka could tell what was going to happen. She stood at the back and watched the dealer bid for the disk. Up and up went the price, until finally the other bids fell away and the auctioneer slammed down the gavel and pointed to the dealer.

On her way out of the school, Merkka saw Dad leaning against Charlie's truck talking with Ed Ingalls.

"They sold Bob Brackett's pinwheel rake thing," Merkka told him.

Dad nodded. "Ed and I helped fetch it here."

"Why?" She looked from one to the other. "What for?"

"For your grandmother," Ed Ingalls told her.

Dad said, "Ma will never finish mending those disks. I don't think Bob'll mind us selling one this way. It'll probably pay for a mower-conditioner and a fleet of rakes besides."

"Does Gramary know?"

"Not yet. Merkka, would you go down to get Ben? He wants to see some of the auction, and Mom doesn't think he should be here by himself with all these strangers from away."

Merkka started down to Water Street. Her mind was on this crazy auction, but she glanced as always toward *Little Mary*'s mooring, noting the wind shift since morning. While she waited for Ben to go to the bathroom and put on his jacket, she told Mom what was going on at the school.

Mom put Caroline over her shoulder before she spoke. "Getting even," she said. "All of them."

Merkka and Ben arrived at the auditorium in time to see

Charlie Budge up front again having a few words with the auctioneer. Oh, no, thought Merkka, certain that something dreadful would come of it. The auctioneer announced that there was one final important Mary Weir object to be offered, and he already had an opening bid from Mrs. Cope. She intended to buy the figure of the upturned boat hull resting near the old steamboat landing. "The name of the vessel is *Dogfish,*" he went on to tell the stunned audience. "Mrs. Cope informs me that if she succeeds in this bidding, she will give *Dogfish* to the town for a museum."

At first there was absolute silence. Perhaps people couldn't believe that the auctioneer really was referring to Gramary's busboat. The auctioneer commenced with Mrs. Cope's bid. A good deal of bidding went on before it narrowed down to two competitors, Mrs. Cope and Mr. Harley Sprague.

Ben tugged at Merkka until she leaned down to him. "I thought Mr. Sprague didn't like Gramary's busboat," he whispered.

"He doesn't," Merkka answered. "He probably doesn't want it there being a museum."

The price climbed higher and higher. Everyone was quiet, attentive. Then all of a sudden Mrs. Cope quit. The busboat belonged to Mr. Sprague.

Ben kept asking Merkka what had happened. How could she explain? It was hard for her to register anything more than that Mrs. Cope didn't look too disappointed that she had lost to Mr. Sprague. Charlie, meanwhile, looked as though he had just won the world. So did most of the town of Ledgeport. Everyone cheered and clapped for all they were worth.

Later Merkka took Ben to Dad in time to hear him telling Mr. Sprague that there was no hurry about moving *Dogfish.* Mr. Sprague didn't seem to know how to respond. Dad spoke easily, gently. On the other hand, he said, if Mr. Sprague intended to leave it in its present location, they might sit down sometime soon to discuss rental of that prime waterfront space.

Mr. Sprague's face changed color. Merkka couldn't hear his muttered reply as he walked away.

CHAPTER 27:

Taken by Storm

*Then the storm came, just the way I had always known
it would.*

*Ed Ingalls used to talk about Gramary in the old
days. One thing he said kept coming back to me. It was
about how Grampa had taken Gramary by storm. That
was when he was a stranger in Ledgeport and took up
with Gramary just because they both had the same last
name.*

*I imagined a wind coming on very sudden and hard,
the way it does sometimes when it veers around to the
northeast. I imagined the sky going bright black and the
sea making up under it. The kind of change that starts
you shivering.*

*When a storm comes like that and dies down
afterward, you feel all clean and strong. And safe.
Sometimes, though, just when you think the storm is*

*past it catches you unaware. That can happen no
matter how much you may know beyond the bounds of
ordinary knowledge.*

*Gramary must have understood that years ago,
maybe when Grampa first came to Ledgeport, or maybe
when he came home from the war hurting and drinking.
If you're a fisherman like her father, Benjamin, who
could spell the herring into his weir, or if you're like
Gramary herself or like Dad, you keep going to sea as
long as you can. And if your house is built on pilings
over the water, you go on living there as best you can.
Until the final storm. Until the final tide comes and
sweeps everything out from under you.*

*When that storm came, we knew something big was
on the way, because there was all this talk on the radio
forecast about the rare alignment of the sun and moon
and earth. Coastal areas were warned about extreme
tides.*

*That night we were supposed to go to the Leewards,
only Gramary sent Charlie after me instead. Mom said
there was room for me with Darleen, but Charlie
insisted. He said Gramary wanted me with her.*

*So I went with Charlie. We took Jet and stopped at the
barn to look at the newborn lambs before going to the
house for the night. I figured that Gramary wanted me
there at Limeburner Point with her because she knew
what no one else guessed about me. She knew how much
I feared the storm.*

*Charlie gave her all the news. He told her Dad and Ed
and Norm were going to sit out the storm in the boat
shed. They had everything lashed down as tight as they*

could, but they were staying anyway, just in case there was something more they could do when things got worse. And a good thing too. We found out afterward how bad it was. In spite of the breakwater, the sea beat against the wharves. It pounded the wreck and it broke across the moored boats. Then there was a lull. Dad and the others went out to secure the crane that had busted loose. They went back inside and drank cold coffee.

Outside the boat shed the sea swelled and swelled. By morning Water Street was flooded. Dad's bait shack floated off. They found it later that day, with barrels still inside it, fetched up in Weir Cove. But Ed Ingalls lost his float, and part of the wharf was damaged. The good things were that Norm's dragger held to its mooring. Our flimsy house held too. Dad thought it held because it offered so little resistance. Still, the downstairs was awash, Mom's new kitchen floor tiles all over the place. The Hudson car seat was ruined and had to be thrown out. It was awhile before we could move back.

Out on Limeburner Point things were different. Charlie's place was higher up and well away from the shore. So they felt safe.

Still Merkka stayed up with Gramary until they thought the worst was over. Gramary sat in her bed in what used to be the dining room and tried hard to make Merkka understand. "Mary Weird," she mumbled, "Mary Weird." She pronounced it like herring weir, as in *dared*. Merkka knew that Gramary wanted to say more than her name. She tried out rhymes inside her head: bared, stared, glared. When she came to scared, she stopped. Mary scared!

But Merkka was on dry land. She didn't feel scared anymore.

"It's all right," she told Gramary. "I'm all right." Then, because suddenly she wasn't at all sure which Mary Gramary had meant, she said, "We're all right."

Charlie woke Merkka up. She couldn't tell what time it was because of the dull gray rain outside and because she had stayed awake so late last night. Charlie told her Gramary had had another turn. The telephone wasn't working. He had to go for the doctor.

Merkka tried to rouse herself. It was hard to shove Jet away and throw back the covers. "What should I do?"

"Just stay with her. Don't make her try to talk."

Merkka pulled on her jeans and her sweater and padded downstairs barefoot. Gramary was lying on her side, her knees pulled up, her back round. She looked like something that might blow away in the wind.

Don't make her try to talk.

Merkka climbed onto the bed and pulled a blanket over her. Jet jumped up beside her. There was plenty of room at Gramary's feet.

Gramary made a sound. It came from somewhere deeper than her throat.

"Charlie said not to talk," Merkka told her.

The sound forced its way up and out of Gramary's mouth. She wanted something.

Merkka, afraid of upsetting her, scrambled off the bed and went to fill Gramary's cup with ginger ale. But when she brought it to her, Gramary only turned her head a little, and her mouth sagged open and drizzled.

The sound came again while Merkka was struggling to prop Gramary's head up. Merkka was using her whole body to push the pillow that would raise Gramary enough so that she could drink. Merkka was still partway behind and partway under when Gramary let out a sigh and with it the reek of urine.

For a moment Merkka was afraid to move. It was as if she herself had spilled that urine by pushing Gramary. She heard her voice tell Gramary never mind, soon Charlie would be back and they would get Gramary all cleaned up and comfortable. A picture of Mom deftly wiping off Caroline's tiny bottom and wrapping her in a fresh dry diaper lay like a film over Gramary lying helpless in her own wetness.

Think of Gramary before the storm, Merkka commanded her mind. Gramary in overalls and her welding helmet; Gramary heading for the mooring, knowing by instinct the moment to shut down the throttle and reach for the mooring buoy. Putting the *Little Mary* to bed, that's what they called it. To bed in the harbor. Think of that, Merkka told herself, her arms around the pillow that held Gramary's head. *Little Mary* secured by a stout line. I'm the mooring, thought Merkka. She began to sing "Rocked in the Cradle of the Deep."

Jet lay curled, head to tail, at the foot of the bed. He didn't stir. Except for Merkka's voice, there was a stillness all around them, the wind down, the risen tide unheard.

When Charlie opened the door and kicked off his boots and the doctor came past him, walking swiftly into the dining room, Merkka was still rocking Gramary and singing another hymn. She sang with care, even though Gramary was home now, safe from the restless wave. Merkka kept on singing, just as Gramary would have done, "for those in peril on the sea."